The New York Times

IN THE HEADLINES

# Climate Refugees

HOW CLIMATE CHANGE IS DISPLACING MILLIONS

THE NEW YORK TIMES EDITORIAL STAFF

Published in 2019 by New York Times Educational Publishing
in association with The Rosen Publishing Group, Inc.
29 East 21st Street, New York, NY 10010

First Edition

**The New York Times**
Alex Ward: Editorial Director, Book Development
Heidi Giovine: Administrative Manager
Phyllis Collazo: Photo Rights/Permissions Editor
Brenda Hutchings: Senior Photo Editor/Art Buyer

**Rosen Publishing**
Greg Tucker: Creative Director
Brian Garvey: Art Director
Megan Kellerman: Managing Editor
Marcia Amidon Lusted: Editor

**Cataloging-in-Publication Data**
Names: New York Times Company.
Title: Climate refugees : how climate change is displacing millions /
edited by the New York Times editorial staff.
Description: New York : The New York Times Educational Publish-
ing, 2019. | Series: In the headlines | Includes glossary and index.
Identifiers: ISBN 9781642820102 (pbk.) | ISBN 9781642820096
(library bound) | ISBN 9781642820089 (ebook)
Subjects:  LCSH: Human beings—Effect of climate on—Juvenile
literature. | Climatic changes—Juvenile literature. | Environmental
degradation—Juvenile literature.
Classification: LCC GF71.C566 2019 | DDC 363.738'74—dc23

*Manufactured in the United States of America*

**On the cover:** South Tarawa, Kiribati, from the air; Josh Haner/
The New York Times.

# Contents

**CHAPTER 2**

# People in Peril

**CHAPTER 3**

# Forced Migration

CHAPTER 4

# Planning for an Uncertain Future

# Introduction

Many people are still debating whether or not global warming, or to use a more accurate term, climate change, is taking place. However, evidence of changes to the climates and weather of the world are taking place every day. Some regions of the world are becoming warmer and drier. Others are experiencing unusually cold winters. Ocean waters are warming, bringing more severe storms such as hurricanes and cyclones. Heavier rains bring flooding, and lighter precipitation causes droughts. Since 1990, single-day weather events that include heavy rains have become more common. While many places are experiencing extreme swings in temperature, with unusually cold winters and very hot summers, the record highs are becoming more common. According to the Environmental Protection Agency, average temperatures have risen across the United States since 1901, and all of the top 10 warmest years on record around the world have occurred since 1998.

These rapidly changing weather and climate conditions are not only difficult to deal with in terms of damage to structures, impact on agriculture and threat to health. In some parts of the world, people can no longer survive in these new conditions. This is especially true of people who rely on agriculture for survival, if they live in an area which is slowly becoming desert due to drought, or in coastal areas that are prone to flooding. Either because of famine or the destruction of property, people and families are being forced to leave the places they call home and seek better conditions elsewhere.

We are used to the term "refugees" being used for people who flee from wars, violence or genocide. However, the term "climate refugees" now applies to those who are forced to leave an area that is

Matthew Mitchell rides a bicycle along the Battery after Hurricane Matthew hit the South Carolina coast October 8, 2016 in Charleston, S.C. The hurricane claimed four lives in the United States.

either threatened or has felt the impact of changing climate and weather, to the point where normal life has become impossible.

The increasing number of climate refugees, plus the scientific research that indicates there may soon be even more of these refugees in the future, creates difficult issues. Where will people move to? Will the time come when even some U.S. states become unlivable? How can existing countries handle an influx of people who will require housing, food and jobs? How can we predict what places will become uninhabitable in the next decades? Can anything be done to help people remain in their homes and their ancestral countries? These are questions that will be asked more often from now on, and these are issues that will become a regular part of the news media and everyday life.

The articles collected here address the conditions that are already driving people away from their homes, the state of climate refugees now and what may happen going forward. By exploring what is taking place, perhaps we will be able to see patterns, understand what works and what doesn't work, and better plan for the future that is coming, whether we believe in it or not.

# CHAPTER 1

# Just the Beginning

Climate change is no longer something that might happen in the future. It is happening now. Whether the effects are rising seas, warming temperatures or droughts, they are creating increasingly difficult conditions. As the climate changes and weather patterns shift, many places in the world are already threatened. Every day, people are weighing the consequences of staying against those of leaving, with neither option promising a long-term solution.

## In Bangladesh, a Flood and an Efficient Response

BY K. ANIS AHMED | SEPT. 1, 2017

DHAKA, BANGLADESH — After two weeks of flooding, about half of Bangladesh is under water, 140 people have been killed, tens of thousands of families have been forced from their homes and well over a million acres of crops have been destroyed. The poorest, their rural livelihoods in ruins, will most likely have no choice but to head to the cities.

As experts attribute the frequency of immense floods to climate change, the thousands who move to Dhaka, the capital, and other cities should be considered climate refugees.

The floods have disrupted life in Dhaka, a megacity that is home to 16 million people. Roads turned into canals. Some people took to using boats. Some waded through waist-high water.

Dhaka is packed with an estimated 135,000 people per square mile and is already the densest metropolis in the world. Its creaky infrastructure can barely support the existing population. The arrival of thousands of flood victims will strain services further.

The August flood is being compared with two other major floods in the country: one in 1988, which resulted in more than 2,000 deaths; and another in 1998, which killed more than 1,000. The fewer deaths this time signify the country's increasing capacity to cope with floods. The same floods have taken more lives in the more sparsely populated areas of neighboring India and Nepal.

Bangladesh's history of frequent flooding and subsequent losses have led to greater investment in flood management. Public schools and mosques are built with a view to their potential use as shelters. Mobile phones, exceeding 100 million, have turned into an important tool for conveying information during a calamity. Bangladesh's government was quick to deploy the army, its soldiers being best equipped to reach remote villages and help with evacuation.

The August floods were caused primarily by overflow from the Brahmaputra River, which flows from northeastern India into northern Bangladesh. Shafiqul Islam, an acquaintance from the northern district of Dinajpur, told me that his father had never seen water rise so fast or so high in their village.

Monira Parvin, his wife, sought refuge with their 5-year-old daughter at her parents' village in a dry area. Ms. Parvin is studying for an undergraduate degree, and her husband, who never made it to a college, proudly supports her. She represents a new generation of educated Bangladeshis, who are more aware of emergency practices such as timely flight to safety.

In previous floods, the destruction of agriculture caused acute food shortages. Since 2010, Bangladesh has become a food-surplus state; because of its grain reserves, there is little risk of the food scarcity of the past.

The most pressing concern for the victims of the flood is their reduced purchasing power. Prime Minister Sheikh Hasina has promised to offer each affected family 30 kilograms of rice at one-fifth the market price. There are other extensive agricultural and social safety support programs in place to help the victims.

There is a limit, though, to what Bangladesh can do by itself. Floods are a transnational affair, and when the big river systems running across China and India and then pouring into Bangladesh go into their seasonal churn, borders mean little. During the floods this time, 800 Indians from the state of West Bengal bordering Bangladesh sought shelter in Lalmonirhat, a northern district of Bangladesh.

India has erected a forbidding barrier of concertina wire along the thousands of miles of border between the two countries. Indian border guards routinely shoot Bangladeshis attempting illegal crossings and kill 50 or more every year.

The Bangladesh border guards, however, did not try to prevent the Indians from crossing to escape the floods. The Indians are reported to have found shelter not just on streets, but also in Bangladeshi homes. A local resident said they "stood by the flood-affected Indians." Common sense and humanity prevailed over jingoism and xenophobia on the India-Bangladesh border.

The increasing frequency and intensity of floods point to the need for cross-border cooperation on shared rivers. India, being both the bigger country and the one upriver, has to take the lead. That means signing water-sharing agreements, which have been pending for two decades. It also means rethinking India's frighteningly dangerous river-linking project that harks back to an era of grandiose development schemes.

If South Asia cannot work together on shared natural resources, it will be ill equipped to cope with the desperate rush of refugees. Going forward, climate change will displace millions — and there is no concertina wire strong enough to hold back multitudes desperate to survive.

# Swallowed by the Sea

OPINION | BY NICHOLAS KRISTOF | JAN. 19, 2018

KUTUBDIA, BANGLADESH — Anyone who doubts climate change should come to this lovely low-lying island, lapped by gentle waves and home to about 100,000 people. But come quickly, while it's still here.

"My house was over there," said Zainal Abedin, a farmer, pointing to the waves about 100 feet from the shore. "At low tide, we can still see signs of our house."

Already much of Kutubdia has been swallowed by rising seas, leaving countless families with nothing. Nurul Haque, a farmer who lost all his land to the ocean, told me that he may have to pull his daughter, Munni Akter, 13, out of eighth grade and marry her off to an older man looking for a second or third wife, because he has few financial options left to support her.

"I don't really want to marry her off, because it's not good for girls," he said glumly. "But I'm considering it." He insisted that if it weren't for the rising waters and his resulting impoverishment, he wouldn't think of finding a husband for her.

One of the paradoxes of climate change is that the world's poorest and most vulnerable people — who contribute almost nothing to warming the planet — end up being most harmed by it.

Bangladesh is expected to be particularly badly hit by rising oceans because much of the country is only a few feet above sea level.

"Climate change is destroying children's futures," noted Justin Forsyth, the deputy executive director of Unicef. "In Bangladesh, tens of millions of children and families are at risk of losing their homes, their land and their livelihoods from rising sea levels, flooding and increased cyclone intensity."

Forsyth said the average Bangladeshi produces just one-tenth of the global average in annual per-capita carbon emissions. In contrast, the United States accounts for more than one-quarter of cumulative carbon emissions since 1850, more than twice as much as any other country.

If Munni is pulled out of school and married off, she'll have plenty of company. Unicef data suggest that 22 percent of girls in Bangladesh marry by the age of 15, one of the highest rates in the world.

"Climate changes appear to be increasing the numbers of girls who are forced to marry," a three-year academic study in Bangladesh concluded.

A year ago in Madagascar I met a family ready to marry off a 10-year-old girl, Fombasoa, because of a drought linked to climate change. And there are increasing reports that poverty linked to climate change is leading to child marriage in Malawi, Mozambique and other countries.

In Kutubdia, climate change is not the only issue. The seas are rising, but in addition, Kutubdia itself seems to be sinking.

The upshot is that the island's shoreline has retreated by about a kilometer since the 1960s, farmers say. Even when land is mostly dry, occasional high tides or storm surges bring in saltwater that poisons the rice paddies.

Thousands of climate refugees have already fled Kutubdia and formed their own neighborhood in the mainland Bangladeshi city of Cox's Bazaar.

A similar injustice is apparent in many poor countries. "Climate change contributes to conflict," noted Neal Keny-Guyer, the C.E.O. of Mercy Corps, the aid group. He observed that a drier climate is widely believed to have caused agricultural failures, tensions and migrations that played a role in the Syrian civil war, the Darfur genocide and the civil war in northeastern Nigeria.

Aside from reducing carbon emissions, Keny-Guyer said, Western countries can do much more to build resilience in poor countries. That can include supporting drought-resistant or saltwater-resistant crops, and offering microinsurance to farmers and herdsmen so that a drought does not devastate them. Mercy Corps is now developing such microinsurance.

The evidence of climate change is increasingly sobering, with the last four years also the hottest four years on record since modern record-keeping began in the 1880s.

We're also coming to understand that climate change may wreak havoc, changing ocean currents, killing coral reefs and nurturing feedback loops that accelerate the warming. It turns out that 99 percent of green sea turtles hatched in the northern Great Barrier Reef are now female because their sex is determined by temperature.

Most of the villagers I spoke to both in Madagascar and in Bangladesh had never heard of President Trump. But the outlook for their descendants may depend on the actions he takes — and his withdrawal from the Paris climate accord is an unhelpful surrender of American leadership.

Americans were recently horrified by a viral video of a starving polar bear, whose condition may or may not be linked to climate change. Let's hope we can be just as indignant about the impact of climate change on children like Munni.

# Living in China's Expanding Deserts

BY JOSH HANER, EDWARD WONG, DEREK WATKINS
AND JEREMY WHITE   |   OCT. 24, 2016

IN THE TENGGER DESERT, CHINA — This desert, called the Tengger, lies on the southern edge of the massive Gobi Desert, not far from major cities like Beijing. The Tengger is growing.

For years, China's deserts spread at an annual rate of more than 1,300 square miles. Many villages have been lost. Climate change and human activities have accelerated desertification. China says government efforts to relocate residents, plant trees and limit herding have slowed or reversed desert growth in some areas. But the usefulness of those policies is debated by scientists, and deserts are expanding in critical regions.

Nearly 20 percent of China is desert, and drought across the northern region is getting worse. One recent estimate said China had 21,000 square miles more desert than what existed in 1975 — about the size of Croatia. As the Tengger expands, it is merging with two other deserts to form a vast sea of sand that could become uninhabitable.

Jiali lives in an area called Alxa League, where the government has relocated about 30,000 people, who are called "ecological migrants," because of desertification.

Across northern China, generations of families have made a living herding animals on the edge of the desert. Officials say that along with climate change, overgrazing is contributing to the desert's growth. But some experiments suggest moderate grazing may actually mitigate the effects of climate change on grasslands, and China's herder relocation policies could be undermining that.

Officials have given Jiali and her family a home in a village about six miles from Swan Lake, the oasis where they run a tourist park. To get them to move and sell off their herd of more than 70 sheep, 30 cows and

Liu Jiali, 4, lives in the Tengger.

eight camels, the officials have offered an annual subsidy equivalent to $1,500 for each of her parents and $1,200 for a grandmother who lives with them.

Residents who live on the edge of the deserts try to limit the steady march of the sand. Along with local governments, they plant trees in an effort to block the wind and stabilize the soil.

Many people in this area are from families that fled Minqin, at the western end of the Tengger Desert, during China's Great Famine from 1958 to 1962, when tens of millions died.

Guo Kaiming, 40, a farmer who also manages a tourist park at the edge of the Tengger Desert, planted rows of trees by a new cross-desert highway in June.

The government encourages farmers like Mr. Guo because it says agriculture can help reclaim land from the desert. Officials offer subsidies: Mr. Guo gets $600 per year for "grassland ecological protection."

Guo Kaiming stands with saplings he planted to help hold back the sand.

But farming is also becoming more difficult. Huang Chunmei, who grew up in the town of Tonggunao'er and now farms there, said the water table was two meters, or about six feet, below ground during her childhood, and "now, you have to dig four or five meters."

Ms. Huang planted more than 200 trees on her own last spring, in the hope that they would help block sandstorms and hold back the sand.

About 17 percent of the population in Alxa League are ethnic Mongolians, whose lives and livelihoods have long been tied to the herding the government is trying to halt.

Mengkebuyin, 42, and his wife, Mandula, 41, grow corn and sunflowers, but their 200 sheep provide most of their income: They sell the meat to a hotel restaurant in a nearby city.

The sheep graze in the desert, where grass is growing scarce. They roam by his old family home, near the shores of a lake that dried up years ago. Mengkebuyin and his wife maintain the old home but do not stay for long periods.

Huang Chunmei, 38, works in her garden in the town of Tonggunao'er.

Mengkebuyin and Mandula have decided that they want their 16-year-old daughter to live and work in a city.

Four generations of Mengkebuyin's family lived by the lake in a thriving community. But gradually, everyone left.

The desert has taken over.

# Mexico City, Parched and Sinking, Faces a Water Crisis

BY MICHAEL KIMMELMAN  |  FEB. 17, 2017

MEXICO CITY — On bad days, you can smell the stench from a mile away, drifting over a nowhere sprawl of highways and office parks.

When the Grand Canal was completed, at the end of the 1800s, it was Mexico City's Brooklyn Bridge, a major feat of engineering and a symbol of civic pride: 29 miles long, with the ability to move tens of thousands of gallons of wastewater per second. It promised to solve the flooding and sewage problems that had plagued the city for centuries.

Only it didn't, pretty much from the start. The canal was based on gravity. And Mexico City, a mile and a half above sea level, was sinking, collapsing in on itself.

It still is, faster and faster, and the canal is just one victim of what has become a vicious cycle. Always short of water, Mexico City keeps drilling deeper for more, weakening the ancient clay lake beds on which the Aztecs first built much of the city, causing it to crumble even further.

It is a cycle made worse by climate change. More heat and drought mean more evaporation and yet more demand for water, adding pressure to tap distant reservoirs at staggering costs or further drain underground aquifers and hasten the city's collapse.

In the immense neighborhood of Iztapalapa — where nearly two million people live, many of them unable to count on water from their taps — a teenager was swallowed up where a crack in the brittle ground split open a street. Sidewalks resemble broken china, and 15 elementary schools have crumbled or caved in.

Much is being written about climate change and the impact of rising seas on waterfront populations. But coasts are not the only places affected.

Mexico City — high in the mountains, in the center of the country — is a glaring example. The world has a lot invested in crowded capitals like this one, with vast numbers of people, huge economies and the stability of a hemisphere at risk.

One study predicts that 10 percent of Mexicans ages 15 to 65 could eventually try to emigrate north as a result of rising temperatures, drought and floods, potentially scattering millions of people and heightening already extreme political tensions over immigration.

The effects of climate change are varied and opportunistic, but one thing is consistent: They are like sparks in the tinder. They expose cities' biggest vulnerabilities, inflaming troubles that politicians and city planners often ignore or try to paper over. And they spread outward, defying borders.

Around the world, extreme weather and water scarcity are accelerating repression, regional conflicts and violence. A Columbia University report found that where rainfall declines, "the risk of a low-level conflict escalating to a full-scale civil war approximately doubles the following year." The Pentagon's term for climate change is "threat multiplier."

And nowhere does this apply more obviously than in cities. This is the first urban century in human history, the first time more people live in cities than don't, with predictions that three-quarters of the global population will be urban by 2050. By that time, according to another study, there may be more than 700 million climate refugees on the move.

For many cities around the world, adapting to climate change is a route to long-term prosperity. That's the good news, where societies are willing to listen. But adaptation can also be costly and slow. It can run counter to the rhythms of political campaigns and headlong into powerful, entrenched interests, confounding business as usual. This is, in effect, what happened in New Orleans, which ignored countless warning signs, destroyed natural protections, gave developers a free pass and failed to reinforce levees before Hurricane Katrina left much of the city in ruins.

Unlike traffic jams or crime, climate change isn't something most people easily feel or see. It is certainly not what residents in Mexico City talk about every day. But it is like an approaching storm, straining an already precarious social fabric and threatening to push a great city toward a breaking point.

As Arnoldo Kramer, Mexico City's chief resilience officer, put it: "Climate change has become the biggest long-term threat to this city's future. And that's because it is linked to water, health, air pollution, traffic disruption from floods, housing vulnerability to landslides — which means we can't begin to address any of the city's real problems without facing the climate issue."

There's much more at stake than this city's well-being. At the extreme, if climate change wreaks havoc on the social and economic fabric of global linchpins like Mexico City, warns the writer Christian Parenti, "no amount of walls, guns, barbed wire, armed aerial drones or permanently deployed mercenaries will be able to save one half of the planet from the other."

## SPRAWL AND SUBSISTENCE

An element of magical realism plays into Mexico City's sinking. At a roundabout along the Paseo de la Reforma, the city's wide downtown boulevard, the gilded Angel of Independence, a symbol of Mexican pride, looks over a sea of traffic from the top of a tall Corinthian column.

Tourists snap pictures without realizing that when Mexico's president cut the ribbon for the column in 1910, the monument sat on a sculptured base reached by climbing nine shallow steps. But over the decades, the whole neighborhood around the monument sank, like a receding ocean at low tide, gradually marooning the Angel. Fourteen large steps eventually had to be added to the base so that the monument still connected to the street.

Deeper in the city's historic center, the rear of the National Palace now tilts over the sidewalk like a sea captain leaning into a strong headwind. Buildings here can resemble Cubist drawings, with slanting windows, wavy cornices and doors that no longer align with their frames. Pedestrians trudge up hills where the once flat lake bed has given way. The cathedral in the city's central square, known as

Volcanic soil safeguarded the water supply for centuries.

the Zócalo, famously sunken in spots during the last century, is a kind of fun house, with a leaning chapel and a bell tower into which stone wedges were inserted during construction to act more or less like matchbooks under the leg of a wobbly cafe table.

Loreta Castro Reguera is a young, Harvard-trained architect who has made a specialty of the sinking ground in Mexico City, a phenomenon known as subsidence. She pointed down a main street that stretches from the Zócalo and divides east from west, following the route of an ancient Aztec dike.

The whole city occupies what was once a network of lakes. In 1325, the Aztecs established their capital, Tenochtitlán, on an island. Over time, they expanded the city with landfill and planted crops on floating gardens called chinampas, plots of arable soil created from wattle and sediment. The lakes provided the Aztecs with a line of defense, the chinampas with sustenance. The idea: Live with nature.

Then the conquering Spaniards waged war against water, determined to subdue it. The Aztec system was foreign to them. They replaced the dikes and canals with streets and squares. They drained the lakes and cleared forestland, suffering flood after flood, including one that drowned the city for five straight years.

"The Aztecs managed," Ms. Castro said. "But they had 300,000 people. We now have 21 million."

Mexico City today is an agglomeration of neighborhoods that are really many big cities cheek by jowl. During the last century, millions of migrants poured in from the countryside to find jobs. The city's growth, from 30 square miles in 1950 to a metropolitan area of about 3,000 square miles 60 years later, has produced a vibrant but chaotic megalopolis of largely unplanned and sprawling development. Highways and cars choke the atmosphere with heat-inducing carbon dioxide — and development has wiped out nearly every remaining trace of the original lakes, taxing the underground aquifers and forcing what was once a water-rich valley to import billions of gallons from far away.

The system of getting the water from there to here is a miracle of modern hydroengineering. But it is also a crazy feat, in part a consequence of the fact that the city, with a legacy of struggling government, has no large-scale operation for recycling wastewater or collecting rainwater, forcing it to expel a staggering 200 billion gallons of both via crippled sewers like the Grand Canal. Mexico City now imports as much as 40 percent of its water from remote sources — then squanders more than 40 percent of what runs through its 8,000 miles of pipes because of leaks and pilfering. This is not to mention that pumping all this water more than a mile up into the mountains consumes roughly as much energy as does the entire metropolis of Puebla, a Mexican state capital with a population akin to Philadelphia's.

Even with this mind-boggling undertaking, the government acknowledges that nearly 20 percent of Mexico City residents — critics put the number even higher — still can't count on getting water from their taps each day. For some residents, water comes only once a week, or once every several weeks, and that may mean just an hour of yellow muck dripping from the faucet. Those people have to hire trucks to deliver drinking water, at costs sometimes exponentially higher than wealthy residents pay in better-served neighborhoods.

Overseeing the city's water supply is a thin, patient man with the war-weary air of an old general: Ramón Aguirre Díaz, director of the Water System of Mexico City, is unusually frank about the perils ahead.

"Climate change is expected to have two effects," he told me. "We expect heavier, more intense rains, which means more floods, but also more and longer droughts."

If it stops raining in the reservoirs where the city gets its water, "we're facing a potential disaster," he said. "There is no way we can provide enough trucks of water to deal with that scenario."

"If we have the problems that California and São Paulo have had," he added, "there is the serious possibility of unrest."

The problem is not simply that the aquifers are being depleted. Mexico City rests on a mix of clay lake beds and volcanic soil. Areas like downtown sit on clay. Other districts were built on volcanic fields.

Volcanic soil absorbs water and delivers it to the aquifers. It's stable and porous. Picture a bucket filled with marbles. You can pour water into the bucket, and the marbles will hardly move. Stick a straw into the bucket to extract the water, and the marbles still won't move. For centuries, before the population exploded, volcanic soil guaranteed that the city had water underground.

Mexico City's water crisis today comes partly from the fact that so much of this porous land — including large stretches of what Mexico City has supposedly set aside for agriculture and preservation, called "conservation land" — has been developed. So it is buried beneath concrete and asphalt, stopping rain from filtering down to the aquifers, causing floods and creating "heat islands" that raise temperatures further and only increase the demand for water. This is part of the sprawl problem.

Now, picture layered sheets of plastic. On a molecular level, clay acts sort of like that. It doesn't really absorb water. Instead, water settles between the sheets. When the water is drained, the sheets can collapse and crack. If all of Mexico City were built on clay, it would at least sink at the same rate and "subsidence would be an anecdote," Mr. Aguirre said.

But because the city is built on a mix of clay and volcanic soil, it sinks unevenly, causing dramatic and deadly fissures. In Iztapalapa, Pedro Moctezuma Barragán, director of ecological studies at the Metropolitan Autonomous University, climbed down into what felt like a ravine where a street had given way. He's been tracking the problem for years. Fifteen thousand houses in the area, he said, had been damaged by sinking ground.

## 'THE CENTER OF WOMEN'S LIVES'

Deep below the historic center, water extracted from aquifers now can end up just beyond the city limits, in Ecatepec, at one of the largest pumping stations along the Grand Canal. The pump, completed in 2007, was built to move 11,000 gallons per second — essentially water that now needs to be lifted up from where the canal has collapsed, just so that it can continue on its way.

The man in charge of this herculean undertaking is Carlos Salgado Terán, chief of the department of drainage for Zone A in Mexico City, a trim, no-funny-business official in a starched bright green shirt. According to Mr. Salgado, the Grand Canal today is working at only 30 percent of capacity because of subsidence. He admitted that it was a Sisyphean struggle to keep up with the city's decline. Parts of the canal around Ecatepec have sunk an additional six feet just since the plant was built, he said.

He showed me around one morning. The canal is wide open, a stinking river of sewage belching methane and sulfuric acid. Apartment blocks, incongruously painted cheerful Crayola colors, hug the bank. A lonely tricycle sat in a parking lot near where the station's giant, noisy engines churn out greasy white foam that coats the black water.

Mr. Salgado asked if I wanted a tour of the filters. "The smell can be unbearable, and it's very unhealthy," he cautioned.

The district of Tlalpan is on the opposite side of Mexico City. There, Claudia Sheinbaum, a former environment minister who developed the city's first climate change program, is now a local district president. She has the slightly impatient, defensive mien of someone wrestling with an impossible mission.

"With climate change, the situation will only get much worse," she said. A warming climate will only increase the city's problems with pollution, specifically ozone. Heat waves mean health crises and rising costs for health care in a city where air-conditioning is not common-place in poor neighborhoods. She seconded what Mr. Aguirre had said about the threat of drought. "Yes," she said, "if there is drought we are not prepared."

For the time being, Well 30 helps supply Tlalpan with drinking water. One recent morning, large trucks, called "pipas," some with neat lettering that promised "agua potable," crowded a muddy turnoff beside the highway.

These pipes plunge 1,000 feet down to reach an aquifer. Trucks, endlessly, one after another, wait their turn to fill up, positioning themselves beneath the hoses.

This is where residents of Tlalpan get water when they can't get it from their faucets. It takes more than 500 trips a day to satisfy the parched citizens of the district. Juan José López, the district representative at the well, distributes assignments from a desk in the red building piled with stacks of orders that residents file. Drivers wait at his window, as at a fast-food drive-through, to pick up their assignments.

"The pump is always working," Mr. López said. "At least it is still good water."

To the east, in Iztapalapa, some wells tap into a noxious stew contaminated by minerals and chemicals. Angry residents wait in lines overnight to plead with pipa drivers, who sometimes pit desperate families against one another, seeing who pays the bigger bribe.

Fernando González, who helped manage the water supply for Iztapalapa for 32 years, said the health effects of contaminated water were clear to residents whose infants regularly broke out in rashes and whose grandparents suffered colitis.

In some cases, the wait for water trucks can make the cable guy look punctual: Deliveries may be promised in three to 30 days, forcing residents to stay home the whole time, because orders are canceled if there's no one in the house when the trucks arrive.

"Water becomes the center of women's lives in places where there is a serious problem," points out Mireya Imaz, a program director at the National Autonomous University of Mexico. "Women in Iztapalapa can spend all night waiting for the pipas, then they have to be home for the trucks, and sometimes they will ride with the drivers to make sure the drivers deliver the water, which is not always a safe thing to do."

"It becomes impossible for many poor women to work outside the home," she said. "The whole system is made worse by corruption."

That's pretty much what I heard talking to women in Iztapalapa. Virginia Josefina Ramírez Granillo was standing in the courtyard of a community center in San Miguel Teotongo, a hilly neighborhood on the edge of the district, next to a wishful mural showing a woman washing clothes in her sink with a running faucet.

"We line up at 3 in the morning for the pipa," Ms. Ramírez said, pointing toward a distant spot where the trucks arrive. "We wait for hours to get water that doesn't last a week, and usually there aren't enough pipas.

People in rich neighborhoods on the other side of town, "they don't have to think about water," she added. "But for us it is something we think about all day, every day."

### ONE PIPA, TWO DONKEYS

Finally, there are places in Mexico City that even pipas can't reach, where the precariousness of the entire water system, and by extension the whole city, is epitomized in a few scruffy acres.

Diana Contreras Guzmán lives in the highlands of the district of Xochimilco, where the roads rise almost vertically and dirt byways lead to shanties made of corrugated tin, cinder block and cardboard. A

A boy in Xochimilco washes a machete in pipa water.

young single mother, she lives with nine relatives in a one-room shack. Ms. Guzmán's father and three brothers are janitors. Her sister works in an office. To reach a bus to get to work, more than a mile down the hill, they set out at 4:30 a.m., leaving Ms. Guzmán, most days, to care for four small children — and to deal with water.

Once a week, a pipa delivers water farther up the hill, where the road is paved. When that happens, Ms. Guzmán, a small, thin woman, spends two hours climbing up the hill and back down again, seven times in all, lugging 90 pounds of water on each return trip. Sometimes Josué and Valentina, two of the children, try to help, dragging half-gallon bottles. Ms. Guzmán can't leave the house for long, she said, in case someone steals water from her cistern.

For 100 gallons from the pipa, she pays 25 cents. But this doesn't begin to supply her family with enough water. So every day she also pays Ángel, a neighbor in his 70s who owns a pair of donkeys named Reindeer and Rabbit. The donkeys trudge plastic containers of water, four at a time, from a well down the hill.

Ms. Guzmán's family earns $600 a month. They ultimately have to spend more than 10 percent of that income on water — enough to yield about 10 gallons per person per day.

The average resident in a wealthy Mexico City neighborhood to the west, nearer the reservoirs, consumes 100 gallons per day, experts note. The wealthy resident pays one-tenth what Ms. Guzmán does.

"Is there any clearer indication that everything about water in this city comes down to inequity?" said David Vargas, whose company, Isla Urbana, produces a low-cost rainwater-harvesting system.

I put this question to Tanya Müller García, the city's secretary for the environment. "We're constantly breaking records for the warmest months," she said, handing over a report on Mexico City's sustainability plans. There are predictions that by 2080 the city's average temperature will have risen several degrees and that annual rainfall will have decreased 20 percent.

JOSH HANER/THE NEW YORK TIMES

Donkeys deliver water in some areas not served by pipas.

Ms. Müller was defensive about the city's inability to supply every resident with clean water, insisting that the numbers of those unserved were exaggerated. She listed progressive new programs intended to combat pollution, preserve green spaces and reduce the demand for cars by improving mass transit. This city is full of brilliant people with good ideas, including a plan to create a water fund into which corporations drawing heavily on the water supply would pay — to help improve services in less advantaged areas. Another plan envisions a public park that would double as a rainwater collection basin. And there's a long-term agenda to turn the airport into a green, mixed-use district.

Meanwhile, the Mexican federal government envisions constructing a giant new airport on a dry lake bed, exactly the worst place to build. It recently cut to zero federal money budgeted for fixing the city's pipes, Metro and other critical infrastructure. Partly this is just politics. The mayor of Mexico City has talked about running for president. The current administration doesn't want to do him any favors. At the same time, the federal government has its own agenda, promoting highways, cars and sprawl.

The disconnect between local and federal officials is not unique to Mexico. Often big cities find themselves undermined by state and federal politicians catering to a different electorate, as if in the end the consequences won't be ruinous for everyone.

"There has to be a consensus — of scientists, politicians, engineers and society — when it comes to pollution, water, climate," Ms. Sheinbaum, the former environment minister, stressed. "We have the resources, but lack the political will."

It turns out Ms. Sheinbaum herself lives in a house that can count on water from the tap only twice a month. So she, too, orders pipas to come to fill her cistern.

# Polar Bears' Path to Decline Runs Through Alaskan Village

BY ERICA GOODE  |  DEC. 18, 2016

KAKTOVIK, ALASKA — Come fall, polar bears are everywhere around this Arctic village, dozing on sand spits, roughhousing in the shallows, padding down the beach with cubs in tow and attracting hundreds of tourists who travel long distances to see them.

At night, the bears steal into town, making it dangerous to walk outside without a firearm or bear spray. They leave only reluctantly, chased off by the polar bear patrol with firecracker shells and spotlights.

On the surface, these bears might not seem like members of a species facing possible extinction.

Scientists have counted up to 80 at a time in or near Kaktovik; many look healthy and plump, especially in the early fall, when their presence overlaps with the Inupiat village's whaling season.

But the bears that come here are climate refugees, on land because the sea ice they rely on for hunting seals is receding.

The Arctic is warming twice as fast as the rest of the planet, and the ice cover is retreating at a pace that even the climate scientists who predicted the decline find startling.

Much of 2016 was warmer than normal, and the freeze-up came late. In November, the extent of Arctic sea ice was lower than ever recorded for that month. Though the average rate of ice growth was faster than normal for the month, over five days in mid-November the ice cover lost more than 19,000 square miles, a decline that the National Snow and Ice Data Center in Colorado called "almost unprecedented" for that time of year.

In the southern Beaufort Sea, where Kaktovik's 260 residents occupy one square mile on the northeast corner of Barter Island, sea ice loss has been especially precipitous.

JOSH HANER/THE NEW YORK TIMES

Polar bears holding each other in waters near the village.

The continuing loss of sea ice does not bode well for polar bears, whose existence depends on an ice cover that is rapidly thinning and melting as the climate warms. As Steve Amstrup, chief scientist for Polar Bears International, a conservation organization, put it, "As the sea ice goes, so goes the polar bear."

The largest of the bear species and a powerful apex predator, the charismatic polar bear became the poster animal for climate change.

Al Gore's 2006 film, "An Inconvenient Truth," which depicted a lone polar bear struggling in a virtually iceless Arctic sea, tied the bears to climate change in many people's minds. And the federal government's 2008 decision to list polar bears as threatened under the Endangered Species Act — a designation based in part on the future danger posed by a loss of sea ice — cemented the link.

But even as the polar bear's symbolic role has raised awareness, some scientists say it has also oversimplified the bears' plight and unwittingly opened the door to attacks by climate denialists.

"When you're using it as a marketing tool and to bring in donations, there can be a tendency to lose the nuance in the message," said Todd Atwood, a research wildlife biologist at the United States Geological Survey's Alaska Science Center. "And with polar bears in particular, I think the nuances are important."

Few scientists dispute that in the long run — barring definitive action by countries to curb global greenhouse gas emissions — polar bears are in trouble, and experts have predicted that the number will decrease with continued sea ice loss. A 2015 assessment for the International Union for Conservation of Nature's Red List projected a reduction of over 30 percent in the number of polar bears by 2050, while noting that there was uncertainty about how extensive or rapid the decline of the bears — or the ice — would be. A version of the assessment was published online Dec. 7 in the journal Biology Letters.

But the effect of climate change in the shorter term is less clear cut, and a populationwide decline is not yet apparent.

Nineteen subpopulations of polar bears inhabit five countries that ring the Arctic Circle — Canada, the United States, Norway, Greenland and Russia.

Of those, three populations, including the polar bears in the southern Beaufort Sea, are falling in number.

But six other populations are stable. One is increasing. And scientists have so little information about the remaining nine that they are unable to gauge their numbers or their health.

In their analysis, the researchers who conducted the Red List assessment concluded that polar bears should remain listed as "vulnerable," rather than be moved up to a more endangered category.

Yet numbers aside, scientists are seeing other, more subtle indicators that the species is at increasing risk, including changes in the bears' physical condition, body size, reproduction and survival rates. And scientists have linked some of these changes to a loss of sea ice and an increase in ice-free days in the areas where the bears live.

Climate-change denialists have seized on the uncertainties in the science to argue that polar bears are doing fine and that sea ice loss does not pose a threat to their survival. But wildlife biologists say there is little question that the trend, for both sea ice and polar bears, is downward. The decline of a species, they note, is never a steady march to extinction.

"It's not going to happen in a smooth, linear way," said Eric Regehr, a biologist at the federal Fish and Wildlife Service in Anchorage who took part in the 2015 assessment and presented the findings at a meeting in June of the International Union's Polar Bear Specialist Group.

A dozen polar bears pick through the bone pile that sits just outside town. Men from the whaling crews had dumped the carcass of a bowhead whale on the pile earlier in the day. As two visitors watch from the safety of a pickup truck a few hundred yards away, the bears devour the leftover meat and blubber.

A bowhead whale that was caught near Kaktovik.

The Inupiat people, who have been whaling here for thousands of years, believe that a whale gives itself to the crew that captures it. Once the animal's body is pulled to shore, water is poured over it to free its spirit.

Even a few decades ago, most polar bears in the southern Beaufort Sea remained on the ice year-round or, if they did come to shore, stopped only briefly. The sea ice gave them ready access to seals, the staple of their high-fat diet.

But as the climate has warmed, the spring thaw has come earlier and the fall freeze later. The pack ice that was once visible from Kaktovik even in summertime has retreated hundreds of miles offshore, well beyond the southern Beaufort's narrow continental shelf. The edge of the pack ice is now over deep water, where seals are few and far between and the distance to land is a long swim, even for a polar bear.

As a result, researchers have found, a larger proportion of the bears in the southern Beaufort region are choosing to spend time on shore: an average of 20 percent compared with 6 percent two decades earlier, according to a recently published study by Dr. Atwood of the Geological Survey and his colleagues that tracked female bears with radio collars. And the bears are staying on land longer — this year they arrived in August and stayed into November — remaining an average of 56 days compared with an average of 20 days two decades ago.

"It's one of two choices: Stay with the pack ice, or come to shore," Dr. Atwood said of the southern Beaufort bears. "If they sit on that ice and those waters are very deep, it will be harder for them to find nutrition."

The shifts that researchers are seeing go beyond where polar bears decide to spend their summers.

In the southern Beaufort Sea and in the western Hudson Bay — the two subpopulations studied the most by researchers — bears are going into the winter skinnier and in poorer condition.

They are also smaller. And older and younger bears are less likely to survive than in the past.

"You see it reflected through the whole population," said Andrew Derocher, a professor of biological sciences at the University of Alberta, who has studied polar bears for 32 years. "They just don't grow as fast, and they don't grow as big."

The proliferation of polar bears in Kaktovik in the fall has drawn wildlife photographers, journalists and climate-change tourists to the village, filling its two small hotels or flying in from Fairbanks for the day on chartered planes.

About 1,200 people came to view the bears in 2015, and the number is increasing year by year, according to Robert Thompson, an Inupiat guide who owns one of six boats that take tourists to view the bears.

Some visitors are surprised at the bears' darkened coats, dirty from rolling in sand and whale remains. "They don't look like polar bears," one man from the Netherlands said. "But it does not matter. I will Photoshop them when I get home."

Susan Trucano, who arrived in early September with her son, Matthew, said they wanted to see polar bears in the wild before they were driven to extinction.

"It was an urgency to come here," Ms. Trucano said. "My fear was that we would lose the opportunity of seeing these magnificent animals."

The increasing tourism has been a financial boon for some people in Kaktovik, but it has upset others. Tourists take up seats on the small commercial flights in and out of the village during the fall months when the bears are there, crowding out residents who need to fly to Anchorage or Fairbanks. And some visitors wander through town snapping pictures without asking permission, or get in the way of the rituals that accompany the whale hunt. Last year, an intrusive tourist nearly came to blows with one of the whaling captains.

For the most part, polar bears and people have coexisted peacefully here. Village residents are tolerant of the bears — "They could break right in here, but they know the rules," said Merlyn Traynor, a proprietor of the Waldo Arms Hotel — and with the whale remains, they have little reason to come after humans.

But as the Arctic ice continues to shrink, bears are arriving in poorer condition and are staying longer, even as the number of tourists increases. Interaction between bears and humans is becoming more common, as it has in other parts of the Arctic, exposing the polar bears to more stress and the people to more danger.

So far, there have been no attacks on humans, but there have been some close calls.

"They never used to come into town, or maybe occasionally, like once a year or so," Mr. Thompson said. "Now they're in town every night."

Polar bear experts say they worry that at some point the number of bears seeking food here will exceed what is available.

"When polar bears are fat and happy and in good condition, they're not that big of a threat," said James Wilder, an expert who recently completed a study of polar bear attacks on humans. "But when they get skinny and nutritionally stressed, you've got to watch out."

Threatened species like lions or wolves face predictable threats: poaching and hunting, or the encroachment of human settlements on their habitat.

But the biggest threat to the polar bear is something no regulatory authority involved in wildlife conservation can address: the unregulated release of carbon dioxide and other greenhouse gases into the atmosphere.

Sport hunting once posed a significant danger to polar bears, greatly shrinking their numbers in some areas until 1973, when an agreement among the Arctic countries restricted hunting to members of indigenous groups, and the populations began to rebound.

Oil spills, pollution and over-hunting still pose some risk. But these dangers pale compared with the loss of sea ice.

For many researchers, the most pressing question is how many days a polar bear can survive on land without the steady source of high-fat nutrition that seals usually provide.

"A bear needs sea ice in order to kill seals and be a polar bear," said Dr. Regehr of the Fish and Wildlife Service. "That's a bottom line."

Some scientists have suggested that the bears might learn to survive on other types of food — snow geese, for example — or that they might learn to catch seals in the water, without relying on the ice as a platform.

But most researchers say that is unlikely.

Such changes usually evolve over thousands of years, said David Douglas, a research wildlife biologist at the Geological Survey, who spoke at the specialists group meeting.

But the loss of sea ice "is taking place over potentially a very rapid time frame, where there may not be a lot of time in polar bear generations to home in on behaviors that could give some advantage," he said.

Much depends on how much of the ice disappears. Under some climate models, if steps are taken to control greenhouse gas emissions, the species could recover. And some evidence suggests that during an earlier warming period polar bears took refuge in an archipelago in the Canadian Arctic.

In Kaktovik, at least for now, whales are providing the bears with an alternative source of food. But dead whale is not a polar bear's preferred cuisine.

"The bears are not here because we hunt whales," said Mr. Thompson. "They're here because their habitat has gone away, and it's several hundred miles of open water out there."

# A Remote Pacific Nation, Threatened by Rising Seas

BY MIKE IVES  |  JULY 2, 2016

Climate change is threatening the livelihoods of the people of tiny Kiribati, and even the island nation's existence. The government is making plans for the island's demise.

TARAWA, KIRIBATI — One clear bright day last winter, a tidal surge swept over an ocean embankment here in the remote, low-lying island country of Kiribati, smashing through the doors and windows of Betio Hospital and spewing sand and debris across its maternity ward.

Beero Hosea, 37, a handyman, cut the power and helped carry frightened mothers through the rubble and water to a nearby school.

"If the next one is combined with a storm and stronger winds, that's the end of us," he said. "It's going to cover this whole island."

For years, scientists have been predicting that much of Kiribati may become uninhabitable within decades because of an onslaught of environmental problems linked to climate change. And for just as long, many here have paid little heed. But while scientists are reluctant to attribute any specific weather or tidal event to rising sea levels, the tidal surge last winter, known as a king tide, was a chilling wake-up call.

"It shocked us," said Tean Rube, a pastor with the Kiribati Uniting Church. "We realized, O.K., maybe climate change is real."

Pacific island nations are among the world's most physically and economically vulnerable to climate change and extreme weather events like floods, earthquakes and tropical cyclones, the World Bank said in a 2013 report. While world powers have summit meetings to negotiate treaties on how to reduce and mitigate carbon emissions, residents of tiny Kiribati, a former British colony with 110,000 people, are debating how to respond before it is too late.

Much of Kiribati, a collection of 33 coral atolls and reef islands scattered across a swath of the Pacific Ocean about twice the size of Alaska, lies no higher than six feet above sea level. The latest climate models predict that the world's oceans could rise five to six feet by 2100. The prospects of rising seas and intensifying storms "threaten the very existence and livelihoods of large segments of the population," the government told the United Nations in a report last year. Half of the 6,500-person village of Bikenibeu, for instance, could be inundated by 2050 by sea-level rises and storm surges, according to a World Bank study.

The study lays out Kiribati's future in apocalyptic detail. Causeways would be washed away, crippling the economy; degraded coral reefs, damaged by warming water, would allow stronger waves to slam the coast, increasing erosion, and would disrupt the food supply, which depends heavily on fish supported by the reefs.

Higher temperatures and rainfall changes would increase the prevalence of diseases like dengue fever and ciguatera poisoning.

Even before that, scientists and development experts say, rising sea levels are likely to worsen erosion, create groundwater shortages and increase the intrusion of salt water into freshwater supplies.

In response, Kiribati (pronounced KEE-ree-bas in the local language) has essentially been drawing up plans for its demise. The government has promoted "migration with dignity," urging residents to consider moving abroad with employable skills. It bought nearly 6,000 acres in Fiji, an island nation more than 1,000 miles away, as a potential refuge. Fiji's higher elevation and more stable shoreline make it less vulnerable.

Anote Tong, a former president who pushed through the Fiji purchase, said it was also intended as a cry for attention from the world. "The issue of climate change is real, serious, and we'd like to do something about it if they're going to take their time about it," he said in a recent interview.

But packing up an entire country is not easy, and may not be possible. And many Kiribati residents remain skeptical of the need to prepare for an eventuality that may be decades away.

The skeptics include the rural and less educated residents of the outer islands who doubt they could obtain the skills needed to survive overseas, and Christians who put more faith in God's protection than in climate models. "According to their biblical belief, we're not going to sink because God is the only person who decides the fate of any country," said Rikamati Naare, the news editor at Radio Kiribati, the state-run broadcaster.

As President Tong became a climate-change celebrity, invited to speak at conferences around the world, opponents accused him of ignoring problems back home, such as high unemployment and infant mortality. They derided the Fiji purchase, for nearly $7 million, as a boondoggle; dismissed his "migration with dignity" as a contradiction in terms; and called his talk of rising sea levels alarmist and an affront to divine will.

Mr. Tong, having served three terms, was not allowed to run for re-election this year, but in March elections the opposition defeated his party. The new president, Taneti Maamau, said he planned to shift priorities.

"Most of our resources are now diverted to climate-change-related development, but in fact there are also bigger issues, like population, the health of the people, the education of the people," he said during an interview at Parliament, which sits on reclaimed land at the edge of a turquoise lagoon.

"Climate change is a serious issue, but you can't do very much about it, especially if a big hurricane comes," he added with a hearty laugh.

The Fiji purchase was not the first effort to address Kiribati's perilous future. The World Bank-led Kiribati Adaptation Program, begun in 2003, developed water-management plans, built coastal sea walls, planted mangroves and installed rainwater-harvesting systems. The bank says the project, which cost $17.7 million, has conserved fresh water in Tarawa and protected about one mile of Kiribati's 710 miles of coastline.

But a 2011 government-commissioned report cast doubt on whether the World Bank project helped Kiribati prepare for climate change. And while the mangroves and water management plans have helped, a 2014 study said the first round of sea walls, made of sandbags, had proved counterproductive and caused more erosion.

"Adaptation is just this long, ugly, hard slog," said the study's lead author, Simon Donner, a professor of geography at the University of British Columbia in Vancouver. "The idea that an outside organization can just come in with money, expertise and ideas and implement something easily is naïve. What you need is consistent, long-term funding — the type of stuff that's hard to pull off with development aid."

Denis Jean-Jacques Jordy, a senior environmental specialist at the World Bank, acknowledged that "we had some issues" with the first sea walls but said subsequent ones made of rock were better designed.

There is no shortage of ideas to avert Kiribati's environmental fate. China's construction of artificial islands in the South China Sea shows the promise of sophisticated island-engineering technology, experts say. Mr. Tong commissioned a study on raising Kiribati's coastline.

But such measures are financially unrealistic for a resource-poor, aid-dependent country like Kiribati. "It's not about the place going underwater," Professor Donner said, noting that some of Kiribati's islands had actually grown in recent years because of land reclamation or natural coastal dynamics. "It's about it becoming prohibitively expensive to live in. That's the real challenge for Kiribati."

The parallel freshwater crisis is also fixable, at a cost. Clean drinking water is already scarce on several islands, and saltwater from high ocean tides has infiltrated some wells. Many residents of South Tarawa, home to half the country's people, now get their drinking water exclusively from rainwater tanks. Experts worry that as sea levels rise, Kiribati's fragile groundwater supply will face even greater risks, while the next drought could quickly exhaust the municipal supply and household rainwater tanks. Kiribati could invest in desalinization equipment or ship in drinking water, but this is a country with only one paved road.

"It's all doable," said Doug Ramsay, the Pacific Rim manager at the National Institute of Water and Atmospheric Research in New Zealand. "It's just going to be a very expensive exercise."

Another novel response gaining attention lately is the idea of applying international refugee law — largely drafted after World War II to protect people fleeing political, religious or racial persecution — to those forced from their homes because of climate change.

In 2012, a migrant worker from Kiribati, Ioane Teitiota, applied for asylum in New Zealand, arguing that he was unable to grow food or find potable water in Kiribati because of saltwater intrusion. His lawyer, Michael Kidd, said the distinction between environmental and political refugees was arbitrary. "You're either a refugee or you're not," he said in an interview.

The courts rejected the argument, and Mr. Teitiota was deported from New Zealand last year. Mr. Kidd said he had appealed to the Office of the United Nations High Commissioner for Human Rights.

Still, migration may become increasingly important. Mr. Tong said he hoped to prepare his people to move with job-training programs that would meet standards recognized in Australia and New Zealand.

"The science of climate change is not 100 percent precise," he said in the interview. "But we know without any argument that, in time, our people will have to relocate unless there are very, very significant resources committed to maintain the integrity of the land."

Coastal threats are increasingly clear to residents of Buariki, an oceanside village of thatched-roof huts and towering coconut palms on the island of North Tarawa. Erosion along the beach has already toppled dozens of coconut trees. The World Bank estimates that 18 to 80 percent of the village, which sits on a peninsula not more than a few hundred feet wide, may be underwater by 2050.

Some villagers said they were resigned to leaving. "Our government already has land in Fiji for the Kiribati people, so if there are more high tides here, they'll bring people to live there," said Kourabi Ngauea, 29. "But it depends on the government, and if they can support us."

Others see no need to leave. "This is where I belong," Aroita Tokamaen, 76, said as she peeled a coconut on her patio. "I would rather stay."

The tide that damaged the hospital here last winter was an exceptionally strong king tide, a surge that occurs twice a year when the moon is closest to the Earth. The waves also flooded the thatched-roofed outdoor meeting space of the local branch of the Kiribati Uniting Church.

While some people were alarmed, the pastor, Ms. Rube, said she refused to accept the idea that Kiribati could disappear.

"We are Christians," she said. "So we don't believe that God could have given us this world and then take it away."

REPORTING FOR THIS ARTICLE WAS FINANCED BY THE ACCESS TO ENERGY JOURNALISM FELLOW-SHIP AND DISCOURSE MEDIA.

# Sinking Islands, Floating Nation

OPINION | BY MATTHIEU RYTZ | JAN. 24, 2018

FIVE YEARS AGO, I could not locate the Republic of Kiribati on a map. Yet last month, I spent Christmas with its former president, Anote Tong, and his family in their beautiful ancestral homeland. In just a few years, the citizens of this low-lying Pacific atoll nation have profoundly affected my outlook on our planet and its prospects. The latest climate estimates project that sea levels could rise as much as six feet within this century, threatening to put Kiribati under water.

Over the past few years, I have followed Anote Tong as he has traveled the world to ring the alarm about climate change's dire consequences. Kiribati is a heartbreaking case study for those interested in taking stock of our rapidly accelerating climate woes. The country's carbon footprint is the smallest in the world, and yet it finds itself most gravely affected by a phenomenon it had nothing to do with. Its citizens' fate will eventually be ours, too.

This century will see unprecedented climate-induced migration, and the Kiribati case is merely the beginning. By conservative estimates, some 200 million citizens will be forced to flee their homelands by 2050. Where will we relocate all these climate refugees? For this unfathomable problem, we are now seeing equally unfathomable solutions. One example comes from the Japanese engineering firm Shimizu, which has pitched a futuristic floating-island concept, relying on technology that has yet to be invented, at prices barely any nation could afford (some estimates put an island at $450 billion). As long as we keep recklessly pillaging our planet, we may need to start taking projects like this more seriously.

That's all the more problematic for the people of Kiribati, who cherish their strong connection with their land and the spirits they believe are tied to it. If the island of Kiribati disappears and the people abandon their ancestral homeland, where do the spirits go? Most ethnologists would agree that the land and our immediate environment are intimately connected with language, social organization and culture. A people losing its land in a sense loses itself. Taking that further, Mr. Tong argues that when land disappears, the connection between the physical and spiritual worlds also forever vanishes.

So where to go from here? It's obvious that technological solutions can't and won't save the Kiribati nation (or the rest of us, for that matter). Without major changes, conservation efforts will be in vain. Now the fate of humankind may also soon be beyond repair. Let's not delude ourselves into thinking billion-dollar artificial islands are the solution.

But we have a bigger problem. Our planet needs leaders that can plan 100 years ahead instead of for the next election. But in 2016 Kiribati got a new government whose views on climate change are radically different from its predecessors'.

While there last month, I was detained and interrogated by police and immigration officials. They revoked my visitor permit and confiscated my laptop and projector, in an apparent attempt to prevent me from promoting Mr. Tong's views on climate change. I was able to leave (although my gear remains confiscated), but the Kiribati ambassador to the United Nations tried to prevent the feature documentary from which this short is adapted from premiering at the Sundance Film Festival. (He did not succeed.)

The current president, Taneti Maamau, said in a video presented at the U.N. Climate Change Conference, COP23, in November: "We don't believe that Kiribati will sink like the Titanic ship. Our country, our beautiful lands, are created by the hands of God." The current administration also believes floating islands are a waste of money and is not pursuing them as an option, preferring that climate change funds be used for the economic development for the current islands. Rather than preparing an exit strategy, the new government is focusing on development for the island over the next 20 years, including building the tuna fishing industry, luxury resorts and eco-tourism of previously uninhabited islands and courting investment from multinational corporations. Its vision is to make Kiribati the next Dubai or Singapore.

It makes me wonder whether our political institutions could be more dangerous to our planet's future than climate change itself.

# Left to Louisiana's Tides, a Village Fights for Time

BY TIM WALLACE AND JOHN SCHWARTZ  |  FEB. 24, 2018

JEAN LAFITTE, LA. — From a Cessna flying 4,000 feet above Louisiana's coast, what strikes you first is how much is already lost. Northward from the Gulf, slivers of barrier island give way to the open water of Barataria Bay as it billows toward an inevitable merger with Little Lake, its name now a lie. Ever-widening bayous course through what were once dense wetlands, and a cross-stitch of oil field canals stamp the marsh like Chinese characters.

Saltwater intrusion, the result of subsidence, sea-level rise and erosion, has killed off the live oaks and bald cypress. Stands of roseau cane and native grasses have been reduced to brown pulp by feral hogs, orange-fanged nutria and a voracious aphid-like invader from Asia. A relentless succession of hurricanes and tropical storms — three last season alone — has accelerated the decay. In all, more than 2,000 square miles, an expanse larger than the state of Delaware, have disappeared since 1932.

Out toward the horizon, a fishing village appears on a fingerling of land, tenuously gripping the banks of a bending bayou. It sits defenseless, all but surrounded by encroaching basins of water. Just two miles north is the jagged tip of a fortresslike levee, a primary line of defense for greater New Orleans, whose skyline looms in the distance. Everything south of that 14-foot wall of demarcation, including the gritty little town of Jean Lafitte, has effectively been left to the tides.

Jean Lafitte may be just a pinprick on the map, but it is also a harbinger of an uncertain future. As climate change contributes to rising sea levels, threatening to submerge land from Miami to Bangladesh, the question for Lafitte, as for many coastal areas across the globe, is less whether it will succumb than when — and to what degree scarce public resources should be invested in artificially extending its life.

One sweltering evening last July, almost everyone from around Lafitte gathered near dusk at the bayou's edge to celebrate the expenditure of nearly $4 million of those scarce public resources. There were shrimpers and crabbers, tug captains and roughnecks, teachers and cops. All had come for the ribbon cutting for a grand new seafood pavilion, the latest gambit by the longtime mayor, Timothy P. Kerner, to save the town from drowning.

Free beer sloshed in plastic cups as folks ambled about the cavernous, open-sided shed, sampling shrimp rémoulade and alligator-stuffed mushrooms. Once the politicians had finished flattering one another from the podium, a Cajun band, fronted by a fiddler in a shimmery blue dress, cranked up a rollicking fais-dodo.

Amid the celebration, a fireplug of a man in crisp jeans and a starched white shirt cheek-kissed and bro-hugged his way through the crowd. This was Timmy Kerner's party. In his third decade as mayor, Mr. Kerner had managed to persuade the parish, state and federal governments to pay for his signature showcase at the entry to town.

Timothy P. Kerner, the mayor of Jean Lafitte, at the ribbon-cutting for a seafood pavilion in July 2017.

It might seem counterintuitive to keep building on land that is submerging. But Mr. Kerner did not see it as his job to take a 10,000-foot view. In the years since Hurricane Katrina, he had grown weary of being rebuffed in his quixotic campaign to encircle Lafitte with a tall and impregnable levee. He could rhapsodize all he wanted about preserving his community's authentic way of life. The cost-benefit calculus — more than $1 billion to protect fewer than 7,000 people — always weighed against him.

So he had set out to change it. His strategy was to secure so much public investment for Jean Lafitte that it would eventually become too valuable to abandon. In a decade, he had built a 1,300-seat auditorium, a library, a wetlands museum, a civic center and a baseball park. Jean Lafitte did not have a stop light, but it had a senior center, a medical clinic, an art gallery, a boxing club, a nature trail and a visitor center where animatronic puppets acted out the story of its privateer namesake.

WILLIAM WIDMER FOR THE NEW YORK TIMES

Vanishing wetlands near the east bank of the Mississippi River.

Some of the facilities had been used sparingly, and many at the grand opening questioned whether the seafood pavilion would be much different. To the mayor that was largely beside the point. What mattered was that the structure existed, that its poured concrete and steel beams made Lafitte that much more permanent.

"Do we lose that investment, or do we protect it?" Mr. Kerner asked, barely audible above the din. "I hope people will see that, hey, not only are we fighting hard to exist, but, you know, maybe this place is worth saving."

The sky began to dim over the bayou. "It's such a beautiful place, and it's getting prettier by the day," he said, ticking off his improvement projects. "This is just another step at building the community. It sends a message that we're not going anywhere.

"No matter what, we're not leaving."

### 'WE ARE LITERALLY IN A RACE AGAINST TIME'

Louisiana's "working coast" is dotted with communities that, like Lafitte, may not outlast the people who currently live there: Cocodrie, Delacroix, Dulac, Grand Isle, Isle de Jean Charles, Kraemer, Leeville, Paradis, Pointe-aux-Chenes, Venice.

A fourth of the state's wetlands are already gone, with heavy losses tallied from 2005 to 2008, when the coast was battered in succession by Hurricanes Katrina, Rita, Gustav and Ike. In 2011, the federal government retired 35 place names for islands and bays and passes and ponds that had simply ceased to exist.

State planners believe another 2,000 square miles, or even double that, could be overtaken in 50 years as the land sinks, canals widen and sea levels rise because of climate change. Recent studies show that glacial melting is accelerating in Antarctica and Greenland, driving sea level rise on the Gulf Coast.

Although the recession of Louisiana's coast has slowed somewhat this decade, a football field's worth of wetlands still vanishes every 100 minutes, according to the United States Geological Survey. That is one of the highest rates on the planet, accounting for 90 percent of such losses in the continental United States.

The Gulf Restoration Network, a nonprofit conservation group, calculates that there are currently 358,000 people and 116,000 houses in Louisiana census tracts that would be swamped in the surge of a catastrophic hurricane by 2062. The Geological Survey predicts that in 200 years the state's wetlands could be gone altogether.

"It is the largest ecological catastrophe in North America since the Dust Bowl," declared Oliver A. Houck, a professor of environmental law at Tulane University in New Orleans who has written extensively about land loss in the state.

In addition to the effects of climate change, human engineering has contributed broadly to the losses. Since the early 18th century, the construction of levees on the Mississippi and the closing of its distributaries have altered natural hydrology and stifled land-building silt deposits from spring floods. Property owners and

A swamp near Jean Lafitte in Jefferson Parish. Bald cypress trees are dying off from saltwater intrusion, a result of rising sea levels, subsidence and erosion.

government regulators have allowed the degradation of swamp and marshland, first for farming and cypress-logging and then, more insatiably, for oil and natural gas exploration.

Since prospectors first discovered oil in Louisiana 117 years ago, 57,465 wells have been drilled in 10 coastal parishes, according to the state's Department of Natural Resources. Thousands of miles of canals have been dredged through marshes for access. They broaden each year from erosion caused by boat traffic and storm currents, even as their spoil banks block natural water flow. A 50,000-mile thicket of pipelines connects rigs to refineries and tank farms across the state.

After years of laissez-faire regulation, some consequential finger-pointing has begun in the courts, where parish governments and private landowners are for the first time suing energy companies to rebuild their land. To date that burden has fallen mostly on taxpayers, even when the property being repaired is owned by oil and gas interests, an examination of state records shows.

The impact extends far beyond Louisiana's shoreline. The slender coastal zone, stretching west from Breton Sound across the mouth of the Mississippi to Sabine Pass, contains 37 percent of the estuarine marsh and the largest commercial fishery in the contiguous 48 states. Its ports support 24 percent of the nation's waterborne commerce and a fifth of its oil supply. The coast provides winter habitat for five million migratory waterfowl. Along with man-made levees and flood walls, it is the buffer that keeps the Gulf of Mexico from draining into New Orleans, much of which sits below sea level.

Last year, Louisiana officials acknowledged for the first time that even with a vast restoration program, even with tens of billions of dollars they do not have, they no longer believed they could build land fast enough to offset the losses. Plotted on a map, their projections show 40-mile swaths, encompassing Jean Lafitte and everything below it, splashed in red to denote that, without action, they will disappear within decades. The crisis has become existential, with policymakers confronting choices about which communities they can afford to rescue.

A view of Jean Lafitte along Bayou Barataria. The town is just a couple of miles south of greater New Orleans's fortresslike levee system.

In the starkest illustration, a $48 million federal grant is being used to relocate the nearly 100 residents of Isle de Jean Charles, a narrow spit in lower Terrebonne Parish that has lost 98 percent of its land over 60 years. In a national experiment, the money will be used to buy land and build homes for those willing to move to higher ground on a sugar farm near Houma, about 40 miles north.

To dramatize the state's plight, Gov. John Bel Edwards last year declared the entire coast in "a state of crisis" and successfully lobbied the White House to expedite permits for restoration projects. "The sense of urgency has only magnified," Mr. Edwards said in an interview. "We are literally in a race against time."

Mr. Edwards, a Democrat, insists that his state is "not in full retreat mode," that "the science shows there is a window of opportunity" to sustain portions of the coast. But in a state not known for fiscal oversight, concerns linger about whether good money will be thrown after bad.

"People argue that if you make the investments appropriately it will be fine, and it could be," said Mitch Landrieu, the outgoing mayor of New Orleans. "But nobody really ever has the appetite to have a conversation about cutting off your arms so you can still walk."

## 'IF WE END UP LIVING ON RAFTS, THERE WILL BE PEOPLE LIVING HERE'

The sputter and thrum of boat motors announces the morning along Bayou Barataria well before sunup. Burly men in rubber boots load ice and bait into trawlers moored behind their houses and prepare to push off in the dark.

On a clear day out on the Pen, a four-mile lake that was farmland a century ago, the silhouettes of New Orleans office towers and the Phillips 66 Alliance Refinery are visible to the north and east. Lines of crab traps stretch across the flat water, buoyed with floats painted in their owners' signature colors, like jockeys' silks.

Alligator snouts skim the surface of nearby canals, and a boat's approach sends a blue heron flapping into labored flight.

Jean Lafitte, the pirate and smuggler, patrolled nearby waters before helping to defend New Orleans in the War of 1812, earning a pardon in exchange. Many here trace their lineage back to his day or to the 18th century Acadian settlers whose cuisine and dialect still prevail (although the Frenchman might be confused to hear locals call their home Gene Lafitte).

The people of Lafitte have lived off the water for generations — trapping and skinning muskrats and other marsh dwellers, fishing, crabbing, oystering, building and repairing boats, ferrying workers and supplies to offshore rigs. Many accept the irony that the water may eventually destroy the economy it built.

As it is, cheap imports and domestic farming of shrimp and fish have depressed prices and made it all but impossible to turn a profit. The global oil glut has reduced drilling activity on the coast by almost two-thirds since 2014. Recent graduates of Fisher High are as likely to seek careers in a casino or pharmacy as on a Lafitte skiff, the iconic fan-tailed fishing boats designed here.

Jean Lafitte is laid out for six linear miles along a two-lane road that curves around the east bank of the bayou. Newer houses on land subdivided from a 19th-century sugar cane plantation were built atop six-foot mounds to keep the water at bay. Many older structures have been elevated hydraulically and placed on pillars 10 feet or higher, a process that can cost nearly as much as the house is worth. While government programs pick up some of the expense, there is not enough funding, and some homeowners cannot afford their share, which often exceeds $100,000.

Yet many cannot imagine living anywhere else. They complain that the bloodless cost-benefit formulas determining which communities get protection give little weight to the qualities that make Lafitte desirable (the name Lafitte is used to refer to the town and its adjacent unincorporated areas). Children, they point out, still spend barefoot summers tubing and fishing and training bird dogs to leap off docks.

Kenny Creppel cleaning crabs at Nunez Seafood, a dockside wholesaler in lower Lafitte.

And when they graduate from high school, three-fourths will have been together since prekindergarten.

The policymakers "don't place value on anything but the money, not the longevity of these communities, not the culture," said Tracy Kuhns, 64, a longtime resident of the Barataria community across the bayou from Jean Lafitte. "One of the problems in this country is that people don't have any connection to where they live. People really want that. Why would you take it away from people who already have it?"

Ms. Kuhns, the president of Louisiana Bayoukeeper, an advocacy group for water quality and clean fisheries, pointed out that she did not lock her door (which flies open all day as her 17 grandchildren come and go). There have been but two murders in Jean Lafitte in the past 20 years, compared with 3,829 in New Orleans.

At the center of town sits St. Anthony Catholic Church, which sponsors the Blessing of the Fleet Festival when brown shrimp season opens each spring. The first catch fills the freezers of cousins and neighbors before anything left is sold to Nunez Seafood and other dockside wholesalers.

After a long day on the water, some may wet their whistle with $2.75 Budweisers at Mitch Martin's Welcome Inn, where a swamp-pop band plays on Wednesday nights and gray-haired ladies line dance.

The tavern is run by Timothy and Thomas Wiseman, brothers better known as White Boy and Zabo. Almost everybody in Lafitte has a nickname, some more self-explanatory than others: Skinny Boy, Sandbags, Lunch Meat, Pink Cow. When Tom Wiseman, 52, was a child, someone decided he looked like another guy nicknamed Zabo. "Forty years it has followed me now," he said.

The Wisemans find that the absence of levee protection reinforces the sense of Lafitte as a place apart, for better and worse. "We're outside the line, and they don't care about us," Tim Wiseman, 54, said. "It's always been like that."

"Now we just expect water and damage every five years," his brother said. "It's a way of life."

"And you know what? It still does not make us want to leave," Tim said. "Are we economically feasible? Hell no. But this place will survive. If we end up living on rafts, there will be people living here."

## 'WORST FEELING I'VE EVER HAD.
## NOTHING YOU CAN DO ABOUT IT'

Although only two feet above sea level, Lafitte rarely experienced significant damage from hurricanes until 2005. That year, Katrina's 120-mile-per-hour winds stripped roofs off houses; a month later, Rita sent enough water coursing through lower Jefferson Parish to dislodge whitewashed tombs from graveyards. Homeowners in Lafitte found skulls and an artificial hip among the debris. Together, the storms forced the demolition of more than 150 houses.

There would be more of the same with Hurricanes Gustav and Ike in 2008, Tropical Storm Lee in 2011 and Hurricane Isaac in 2012. With only 2,000 residents, the Town of Jean Lafitte racked up $9.3 million in federal flood insurance payments in the eight years after Katrina, according to an analysis by Rui Hui, a researcher at the University of California, Davis. (Statewide, the program has paid out $19.5 billion in claims since 1978, or 30 percent of the national total, including $1 billion for properties that have flooded repeatedly, according to the Federal Emergency Management Agency.)

"The first time, I sat on the sofa and just watched it come in," remembered Chris Dufrene, 73, whose house flooded three times before he had it elevated eight feet three years ago. "Worst feeling I've ever had. Nothing you can do about it."

Shrimpers and guides had been noticing astonishing changes out on the water for years. Shambles of fishing cabins sat stranded on pilings, more distant from shore each season. Duck blinds had dissolved into muck. Land bridges no longer bridged.

"I've been out here since 1981, and the beaches are eroding, the salt water's intruding and all the islands in Barataria estuary that were protecting the land are washing away," said Troy Schultz, 54, who trawls and crabs with his son, Troy Jr., 28. "Big Island is gone. Cat Island is gone. St. Mary's Island is gone. They were miles long. Now it's so open that every time you get squalls and storms it pulls up the marsh grass."

These days, the main road through Jean Lafitte floods almost any time a gusty storm blows in from the south. A mere sideswipe from Tropical Storm Cindy last June pushed several feet of water into streets and yards. The merciless hurricane season of 2017, with Harvey followed by Irma, Maria and Nate, made clear that the town's days may be numbered.

After Katrina left 1,833 dead in 2005, local, state and federal governments spent more than $20 billion to redesign failed and inadequate levees and pumps for metropolitan New Orleans. Even those improvements may not be sufficient to spare the area's more than 1.3 million residents from another monster storm.

But in Lafitte, only 25 miles south, the hurricane defense system consists mainly of Mr. Kerner and whichever men he can employ to sling tens of thousands of 25-pound sandbags, often for days on end.

The mayor feels the threat viscerally, like many with deep roots here. His family settled in Lafitte in the early 1800s. He married a local girl at 18 (Darla Kerner was 16), and worked as a commercial fisherman, barkeep and tax collector before assuming his place as heir to one of the country's most enduring political dynasties.

Mr. Kerner has been mayor for 26 of his 58 years. With a gap of only eight years in the 1950s, a Kerner has held Lafitte's top office since 1888, when his great-grandfather became justice of the peace. His father, Leo E. Kerner Jr., spearheaded the effort to incorporate Jean Lafitte in 1974 and became its first mayor, serving 17 years.

Leo Kerner had been a welterweight champ in the Navy, and taught his boys how to spar, in politics as in the ring. The current mayor is known in Jefferson Parish, Baton Rouge and Washington as a single-minded scrapper who fights best from a defensive crouch. He can be quick to lose his temper when he feels Lafitte is being disrespected, but is also fast to apologize and hug it out.

Mayor Kerner and others had to prepare for Tropical Storm Cindy by stacking sandbags around residences.

"He's like a big teddy bear," said Susan H. Maclay, president of the Southeast Louisiana Flood Protection Authority — West, which maintains levees on the west bank of the Mississippi. "It's hard to tell him no when he needs help."

Mr. Kerner, a self-described Kennedy Democrat, has made a career of going hat in hand to Republican administrations. He has little choice, as Jean Lafitte's operating budget hovers around $2 million. Legislative audits show that virtually all of the $27 million amassed by Mr. Kerner for construction since Katrina came from federal, state and parish grants. He has lobbied for scores of millions more for bridge and road improvements.

Paradoxically, perhaps, some of the funding — including about a third of the cost of the seafood pavilion — has come from federal recovery grants that flow south each time the town is bludgeoned by a storm.

Residents gathered in a parking lot await instructions from town officials before Cindy moves through the area.

As the water creeps closer, Mr. Kerner has increased the value of Jean Lafitte's physical plant sevenfold in a decade. And yet, on his central mission to ensure his town's future, he considers himself a failure.

"When I ran for this office," Mr. Kerner said, "I ran to provide a levee. That was my dream. I guess I haven't done a very good job so far, because we don't have one."

### 'WHAT DO YOU SUGGEST WE DO?'

If Lafitte has a chip on its shoulder, it is not without cause.

When the Army Corps of Engineers first mapped out Louisiana's hurricane protection system in the 1970s and 1980s, it drew the footprint just north of Lafitte. The priority was to protect New Orleans, its booming West Bank suburbs and Louisiana's ports (the state has five of the country's 12 largest). Feasibility studies repeatedly concluded that extending the levee to defend Lafitte was "not economically justifiable."

That left Mr. Kerner to devise his own plan, and find a way to pay for it. His concept was to phase in the construction of a chain of 10 linked ring levees, 65 miles in all, that would enclose each populated sector of Lafitte. Cost dictated that the walls of dirt, steel and concrete would be seven-and-a-half feet high at the outset, enough for protection from modest storms but not from a major hurricane. A levee of at least twice that height is typically needed to meet the standard of "100-year protection," meaning it should withstand flooding from a hurricane with a 1 percent chance of occurring in a given year.

For a while, the corps encouraged the mayor to pursue small federal grants to build segments of the system. In 2003, with about $10 million, construction began on the first link, which will eventually contain the town's schools and municipal buildings.

Then came Katrina, producing a storm surge that overwhelmed portions of the New Orleans-area levee and flood wall system. In addressing the damage, Congress raised standards for the height and strength of the levees that the Corps of Engineers would build, effectively disqualifying the Lafitte project.

Mr. Kerner also found little support locally, where the regional levee authority with jurisdiction over Lafitte was focused on protecting areas closer to New Orleans. In 2007, David J. Bindewald Sr., then the president of the Southeast Louisiana Flood Protection Authority — West, told Mr. Kerner explicitly that there would be no money for his levees.

Instead, he sent Mr. Kerner a letter offering "several thousand unfilled sand bags and sand sufficient to fill the bags" along with "a quantity of shovels."

The furious mayor figured he could do better than that on his own, and persuaded allies in the Legislature to create the Lafitte Area Independent Levee District. Funded by a small property tax, the levee authority pays Mr. Kerner $12,000 a year as its president, on top of his mayoral base salary of $79,538, according to legislative audits.

Mr. Kerner's power play did not instantly change the essential dynamic. In 2009, after Hurricane Gustav, the corps began studying options for a new levee that would span a stretch of the lower coastal zone. Only one of several routes under consideration would have protected Lafitte. But at a levee board meeting in 2011, corps officials announced their determination that none of the proposed alignments could be justified economically.

"What do you suggest we do?" an exasperated Mr. Kerner asked Mark Wingate, the corps engineer managing the project.

Mr. Wingate said he suggested studying nonstructural options, including relocation. "You're reading my mind," Mr. Kerner responded, "because when I saw that map the first thing I thought was that I wanted to relocate your jawbone." He nodded at Mr. Wingate's two associates. "And your jawbone and your jawbone."

In the parking lot after the meeting, the corps officials stiffened when they saw the pugilistic mayor striding purposefully toward them. But he was only coming to apologize.

### 'THEY JUST BASICALLY SLAP YOU IN THE FACE AND SAY BYE'

Bruised but not defeated, Mr. Kerner thought there might be another way.

Four months after Katrina, the State of Louisiana had created the Coastal Protection and Restoration Authority to centralize planning. The authority was tasked with devising a master plan for the coast, which it did for the first time in 2007, and with updating it every five years. Science, not politics, was to control its deliberations about the most cost-effective ways to protect people and property.

The ambitious 2012 update pledged to use "every tool in the toolbox" to improve flood protection "in every community in coastal Louisiana." It proposed a $50 billion buffet of projects — marsh creation, barrier island restoration, oyster shell reefs, river sediment diversions — that it asserted could start to neutralize land loss over the next 23 years and outpace it by year 30. There also would be billions for house elevations and flood walls — including $870 million to build Mr. Kerner's ring levees at full "100-year" height: 16 feet.

Over the past decade, the authority has grabbed money from a bag of sources to undertake 135 projects at a cost to the state of more than $2.4 billion (with another $2 billion budgeted for the next three years). Sixty-five square miles of land have been built or improved, along with 297 miles of levee and 60 miles of barrier islands and berms, according to the authority.

The coast these days is awash in ambitious engineering projects. Near Jean Lafitte, for instance, more than 1,000 acres of marsh have been created in and around Bayou Dupont in an $82 million state-managed project that pumped sand from the Mississippi up to 13 miles away. Where open water stood in 2009, there is now walkable land, thick with saplings and shrubs.

But before money could be appropriated for the Lafitte levees, the master plan's authors adopted far more pessimistic forecasts of the impact of climate change. They effectively doubled their previous 50-year projections for likely sea level rise to more than two feet, the highest rate in the country, according to the National Oceanic and Atmospheric Administration.

That made the worst-case scenario in the 2012 master plan the best case for 2017 and led to a startling reversal: Louisiana could slow the submergence of the coast, but not arrest it. Even if the plan was somehow fully funded, and the state succeeded in adding or maintaining 800 square miles of wetlands over 50 years, there would still be a net loss of at least 400 square miles and possibly as many as 3,300.

That recalibration necessarily shifted the state's approach. "Once you accept the diagnosis that much of south Louisiana is going to disappear, you still have to have a strategic retreat," said David Muth, director of the National Wildlife Federation's Gulf Restoration Program. "How do you plan this shrinking of the footprint, which is complicated by socioeconomics and by real questions about how fast sea level will rise and how fast you can build wetlands?"

Torbjörn E. Törnqvist, a Tulane geologist who is an authority on subsidence, warned that decisions about places like Lafitte would be "a piece of cake compared to what's coming — because a little down the line we're going to be talking about communities not of 2,000 people but of much bigger things."

And then there's the matter of where to find the master plan's aspirational $50 billion — twice the entire state budget.

To date, the only dependable financing model has been catastrophe, namely the 2010 Deepwater Horizon oil spill. BP and its drilling partners agreed to pay $7.1 billion over 15 years to settle litigation by the state, and the money has been earmarked for coastal restoration. Mark Davis, director of Tulane's Institute on Water Resources Law and Policy, analogizes that to "paying for a gym membership by winning pie-eating contests."

The state and its coastal parishes have been counting on about $176 million a year from federal offshore oil leases under a revenue-sharing law passed in 2006. But steep declines in prices and drilling have lowered those projections.

All told, even under the rosiest circumstances, the $50 billion master plan, which many experts consider inadequate, lacks at least $30 billion in revenue.

"All of us believe our citizens deserve more than probably we can deliver," said Bren Haase, the authority's chief of planning and research.

For its 2017 revision, the authority split its theoretical budget between hopeful restoration efforts, like rebuilding marshes and barrier islands, and defensive risk-reduction projects like raising levees and elevating houses. It re-evaluated proposals with a refined formula that weighed each project's cost against the flood damage it would avert.

The price tag for the Lafitte ring levees had risen to $1.2 billion, equating to more than $170,000 per resident. Despite Mr. Kerner's efforts to rebalance the cost-benefit calculus, the annual savings amounted to less than a tenth of that, placing it near the bottom on the

St. Anthony Catholic Church, at the center of town, sponsors the Blessing of the Fleet Festival when brown shrimp season opens each spring.

state's list. When the authority published its draft in January last year, the mayor found that his ring levees, his lifeline for Lafitte, had been discarded.

The mayor and his constituents felt betrayed once again. "It just makes all your fears justified," said Ray Griffin, the manager of Cochiara's Marina. "When they make a decision like that they just basically slap you in the face and say bye."

### 'WE JUST CAN'T DO THAT. BUT WE HAVEN'T GIVEN UP ON THEM EITHER.'

In an ecosystem as multifaceted as the Louisiana coast, the protection of one habitat may pose a mortal threat to another, or at least be perceived that way. Flood control is a zero-sum game. The water has to go somewhere.

So there is natural suspicion in Lafitte about the most audacious engineering proposal in the state master plan, the $1.4 billion Mid-Barataria sediment diversion. The experimental project, which is under design, would carve a gap in the levee on the Mississippi's west bank just southeast of Lafitte. When the river is high, floodgates could be opened to redirect sediment-rich water into adjoining marshland at up to 75,000 cubic feet per second.

This occasional freeing of the river may build land more gradually than the continual pumping of dredged sand. But environmental groups argue that it will do so in a self-sustaining way at comparatively low cost. The state estimates that the diversion will deposit enough sediment over 50 years to fill the Superdome more than 22 times.

"We know we need benefits now," Mr. Haase said, "but if we're not doing anything to fundamentally change the causes of our land loss, then we're perhaps not investing our dollars wisely."

In Lafitte's fishing community, there is deep concern, with some scientific backing, that flushing fresh water into brackish marshes and bays will imbalance the salinity needed to nurture shrimp, oysters and crab. Scientists argue that salinity will change with or without the diversion, but seafood industry groups have threatened to sue if it is built.

"It will completely kill these fishing communities," said Clinton Guidry, a Lafitte resident who once presided over the Louisiana Shrimp Association. "Is that the trade-off you want? If you lose shrimp fishermen for one generation, they're gone forever."

For Tim Kerner, the Mid-Barataria diversion provided a bargaining chip. After his 100-year levees were axed from the master plan, he continued to push for funds to complete the ring system at lower height. The state owed Jean Lafitte, he argued, because the diversion would make the town even more vulnerable.

Things came to a head in January last year when Mr. Kerner made his case, loudly, at a meeting with state officials. Seated nearby was his great benefactor in Baton Rouge, State Senate

President John A. Alario Jr., a soft-spoken power broker whose district includes Lafitte.

"You know," Mr. Kerner told Johnny Bradberry, the chairman of the Coastal Protection and Restoration Authority, "if I was a senator or a state rep from my area sitting at this table, I would be very upset. You have projects all along the coast, and this area, where the Senate president is from, you have nothing but a sediment diversion that nobody really wants."

He reminded the officials of all of the money the state had been spending in Lafitte — the bridges, the civic center, the seafood pavilion. "It's so inconsistent for C.P.R.A. to say we're not worth saving when other government agencies are spending hundreds of millions of dollars," he said. "It's throwing away the investment of tax dollars you already put in this place."

When the final master plan was presented to the Legislature in June, language had been inserted that the state and the Lafitte levee

Many older structures have been placed on pillars 10 feet or higher, a process that can cost nearly as much as some houses are worth.

authority would be "focused on securing nearly $308 million" for the lower tidal protection levees and flood walls. The plan also called for spending $200 million in Lafitte over 30 years to elevate 1,237 houses, flood-proof nine businesses and buy out two property owners. (Coast-wide, the master plan calls for spending a theoretical $6 billion over 50 years to elevate, improve or buy out 26,200 properties.)

The question now is how quickly money will materialize. Mr. Kerner believes the levees can be completed for considerably less than the $308 million estimate. Regardless, the state has budgeted only $35.5 million for them over the next four years.

"Those 2,000 folks down there would like very much for us to be committed to a $1 billion ring levee," said Mr. Edwards, the governor. "Well, we just can't do that. But we haven't given up on them either."

### 'YOU DON'T BITE THE HAND THAT FEEDS YOU'

Prospects seem dim for a federal bailout to shore up Lafitte and the rest of Louisiana's coast. Preserving the state's wetlands is a tough political sell because many Americans do not appreciate the magnitude of their self-interest there. Increasingly, Louisiana faces competition from more populous coastal zones that also are at grave risk, like South Florida, metropolitan New York and the Texas Gulf.

The only other pockets deep enough to fill the financial gap belong to oil and gas. Even in a time of retrenchment, the energy industry remains among Louisiana's most vital employers, revenue generators and civic and political donors. But with drilling in decline and the BP oil spill a fresh memory, Louisianans seem newly receptive to holding the industry accountable for the consequences of its activities.

In a recent poll of 565 Louisianans by NOLA.com | The Times-Picayune, 72 percent said the oil and gas industry should help pay for coastal restoration along with the government. (Mr. Kerner happens to agree.) Another 18 percent said the industry should bear the cost alone. Only half said they were willing to pay higher taxes to redeem the coast.

In 2013, with the political landscape shifting, the levee authority charged with flood control in New Orleans sued 97 oil and gas companies, presenting a novel claim.

"Everybody understood that the industry was responsible for a significant part of the damage and had placed an increased burden on those responsible for protecting the population from storm surge," said John M. Barry, the New Orleans author who spearheaded the litigation as vice president of the Southeast Louisiana Flood Protection Authority — East. "So it seemed clear there would have to be some avenue to get them to accept their liability."

Over the prior 20 years, plaintiffs' lawyers had won judgments and settlements in Louisiana cases demanding the cleanup of oil field contamination. The flood protection authority hired one of them — Gladstone N. Jones III of New Orleans — and constructed arguments evocative of those used 30 years earlier against Big Tobacco: Energy companies had known for decades that they were destroying the marsh but ignored legal and contractual obligations to repair it, at great cost to taxpayers.

There is considerable documentation of advance knowledge. Scientists and conservationists have sounded alarms since the 1920s about the loss of land to oil exploration. Documents uncovered through discovery show that the industry's own studies began making the connection nearly 50 years ago.

In 1972, a report commissioned by oil and gas transmission companies estimated that pipelines decimated up to two square miles of marsh a year and that access canals destroyed at least that much. Seventeen years later, a study of aerial photographs for the Louisiana Mid-Continent Oil and Gas Association, which represents major producers, concluded that "the direct and indirect effects of canal development tend to be the overwhelming cause of wetland losses." In 2000, a study sponsored in part by the Gas Research Institute estimated that the industry bore responsibility for 36 percent of Louisiana's coastal land loss between 1932 and 1990.

Infrastructure from the oil and gas industry. In August, a federal judge ordered pipeline companies to repair erosion in privately owned wetlands.

More recent research links the industry to subsidence — the compaction and sinking of sediment. "Rapid subsidence and associated wetland loss were largely induced by extraction of hydrocarbons," concluded a 2005 study of the Mississippi Delta plain by the Geological Survey. It added that the collapse of Louisiana's marsh "appears to be unprecedented and not repeated in the geological record of the past 1,000 years."

And yet, some Louisiana lawmakers, both in Congress and the State Legislature, do not support efforts to regulate what may be the most lasting environmental legacy of fossil fuels: climate-driven sea level rise. Among them is Representative Steve Scalise, the House majority whip, whose district includes Lafitte. Mr. Scalise, a Republican, applauded Mr. Trump's announcement in June that the United States would withdraw from the global Paris accord to regulate greenhouse gas emissions.

The state's leadership initially viewed the levee authority lawsuit as a direct assault. The Republican governor at the time, Bobby Jindal, demanded that it be withdrawn and removed Mr. Barry and others on the authority. He orchestrated passage of a law that would have invalidated the litigation had a state judge not declared it unconstitutional.

"It's that old saying — you don't bite the hand that feeds you," said Lt. Gov. Billy Nungesser, also a Republican. "I don't say they have no effect, the canals, but I think it's a money grab against an industry that has been very good to Louisiana."

In 2015, a federal judge dismissed the levee authority lawsuit, primarily on grounds that the agency lacked legal standing. That ruling has been upheld on appeal. But the original lawsuit was followed quickly by scores of others, some filed by private landowners and a total of 43 by six different parish governments (the equivalent of counties).

In August, a different federal judge ruled that pipeline companies must repair erosion that had occurred since 1953 along canals on 20,000 acres of privately owned wetlands in Plaquemines Parish. The first of the lawsuits filed by the parishes is scheduled to be heard in state court in Plaquemines in 2019.

The parishes, all represented by the Baton Rouge firm of Talbot, Carmouche & Marcello, claim that oil and gas companies violated state permitting laws in the dredging of canals, as well as regulations requiring production sites to be "cleared, revegetated, detoxified and otherwise restored as near as practicable to their original condition upon termination of operations." The suits seek actual restoration of degraded land in addition to monetary damages.

In 2016, when the governor's office changed parties, Mr. Edwards reversed Mr. Jindal's stance and intervened in support of the parish cases. "Oil and gas is a huge component of our economy, and we want them to be successful," Mr. Edwards said. "But we also want them to act responsibly when they explore for and produce hydrocarbons."

Oil and gas industry leaders acknowledge that their potential exposure is substantial. They warn they will not roll over to trial lawyers who they believe are extorting them for a global settlement.

"We're going to fight every single last issue because we don't believe we've done anything wrong," said Gifford Briggs, vice president of the Louisiana Oil and Gas Association, which represents independent producers and service companies.

Chris John, a former Democratic congressman who presides over the Louisiana Mid-Continent Oil and Gas Association, said the lawsuits failed to recognize numerous other causes of coastal degradation and would not be settled. He said that "the energy industry has conducted its operations in accordance with government-issued permits and applicable federal, state and local regulations."

Mr. Briggs echoed that defense. "Yes, if you dig a canal or build a slip, is there technically a loss of marsh or land? Sure," he said. "But that's done through permit. That doesn't mean there's any additional liability or responsibility beyond fulfilling the obligations of the permit."

As it is, taxpayers have spent at least $588 million to repair oil-and-gas-related damage in coastal Louisiana, according to an analysis of state records. That accounts for 84 percent of the money spent on more than 200 projects over three decades by the federal Coastal Wetlands, Planning, Protection and Restoration Act. Enacted in 1990, the program is funded by taxes on fishing gear, imported watercraft, boat fuel and motors.

Because petroleum interests own or lease much of the coast, those taxpayer-funded restoration efforts often benefit the very industry that shredded the marsh in the first place. In Terrebonne Parish, for instance, $39 million was spent to repair breaches in a land bridge across north Lake Mechant caused by erosion and oil access canals. Much of the property is owned by Apache Corporation and Louisiana Land and Exploration, both major oil and gas companies, parish records show, and operators have included Conoco Phillips, Texaco and Humble Oil (a precursor of Exxon Mobil).

Jean Lafitte has not yet reached the tipping point when bankers and insurers perceive that the lifetime of their loans and obligations could exceed the lifetime of the town. Indeed, real estate values are relatively high, if only because there is so little to be had.

But there are early signs of an exodus, particularly among younger residents. The population of the area declined by 21 percent between 2000 and 2010, although estimates suggest it has rebounded slightly this decade. Enrollment at the two public schools dropped 27 percent from the peak before Katrina and Rita, but has risen by 10 percent since.

Mr. Kerner believes the declines reflect temporary dislocations. But some, like Buttercup Mancuso, have left for good. She, her husband and three of their children evacuated their rental house in lower Lafitte before it flooded during Hurricane Isaac in 2012. They returned to find mold sprouting two feet up the walls.

The family abandoned their belongings except for their photographs. "Losing everything once was enough for me," Ms. Mancuso, 43, said. "I just couldn't do it again." They moved to the north shore of Lake Pontchartrain, and eventually to North Carolina.

Travis Johnson, 70, a retired Army and commercial helicopter pilot who moved to Barataria in 2000, said that at his age he would gladly take a government buyout for his waterfront house.

"I drove out of here during Hurricane Rita with water flowing over the hood of my Jeep," he said. "Should one delay evacuation, it is not possible to escape. I don't want a lot of complications."

But Lafitte's lifers, for the most part, seem resigned to wait things out. The centuries spent fishing and trapping have built a resilient and self-reliant culture. More than 250 years since the Acadians were expelled from Nova Scotia, there remains a deep resistance to another forced exile.

"People that don't understand it say, 'Why don't you just move away?' " said Ms. Kuhns, the Louisiana Bayoukeeper president, who

Sandbags, stacked and ready in a parking lot in town, make up the majority of Lafitte's hurricane defense system.

refuses to join her daughter, Ms. Mancuso, on the other side of the levee. "The people who are connected to these communities don't think that way. It's a whole culture that's connected to the earth and the water. You can't replicate it."

And so the men sandbag. Last hurricane season, they stacked them by the thousands in anticipation of Tropical Storm Cindy, then unstacked them when the floodwater receded. They did it again for Hurricane Harvey and once more for Nate.

The mayor supervises up and down the road from his white Ford Expedition, crossing himself as he passes the Catholic church. He pitches in long enough to let his back start aching, then carps that it's because the young guys today don't know how to properly swing and catch.

He remembers each storm as a fight, tallying them as wins and losses. In the old days, they would stack 200,000 sandbags. "It was like being in a war zone," Mr. Kerner said. "We wouldn't go to bed for two or three days at a time."

With sections of two of the ring levees complete, the men got by with only 20,000 sandbags when Nate narrowly missed Lafitte last October. "Each time you just have to be ready and fight it as if it's going to be the worst thing that ever happened," Mr. Kerner said. "And then you may have to do it again a week later."

The mayor has developed a sixth sense for the telltale signs of whether Lafitte will flood. As Cindy moved in last June, he watched the tide rising near the Goose Bayou bridge: "That water won't quit," he cursed. "Look at the whitecaps. That's what I don't want to see." Soon the water was lapping at his tailpipe.

Four months later, on the night Nate landed near Biloxi, Miss., he divined better news from the bayou's outward flow, indicating that the leading edge had curled in harmlessly from the north. "That's it," he said. "It's over."

As he drove home, eyelids drooping, Mr. Kerner could not help feeling annoyed that the town had expended so much effort for no reason. Then he remembered that no one had been hurt, no one had been washed out of his or her home or stranded in distress. "Such a relief," he thought.

He eased into bed, bone-weary and sore, like an aging boxer, and lost himself in reveries of shiny new buildings and 16-foot levees — whatever might spare Jean Lafitte from the water, for now.

# CHAPTER 2

# People in Peril

What kind of weather- and climate-related events are taking place around the world with increasing frequency? And how are they affecting the people who must cope with them? From remote Peru to cities like Paris, climate change is beginning to have real effects on people who may not have thought they would ever experience a drought or a flood. And in some cases, the threats from changing climates are just the beginning.

## A Wrenching Choice for Alaska Towns in the Path of Climate Change

BY ERICA GOODE | NOV. 29, 2016

SHAKTOOLIK, ALASKA — In the dream, a storm came and Betsy Bekoalok watched the river rise on one side of the village and the ocean on the other, the water swallowing up the brightly colored houses, the fishing boats and the four-wheelers, the school and the clinic.

She dived into the floodwaters, frantically searching for her son. Bodies drifted past her in the half-darkness. When she finally found the boy, he, too, was lifeless.

"I picked him up and brought him back from the ocean's bottom," Ms. Bekoalok remembered.

The Inupiat people who for centuries have hunted and fished on Alaska's western coast believe that some dreams are portents of things to come.

But here in Shaktoolik, one need not be a prophet to predict flooding, especially during the fall storms.

Laid out on a narrow spit of sand between the Tagoomenik River and the Bering Sea, the village of 250 or so people is facing an imminent threat from increased flooding and erosion, signs of a changing climate.

With its proximity to the Arctic, Alaska is warming about twice as fast as the rest of the United States and the state is heading for the warmest year on record. The government has identified at least 31 Alaskan towns and cities at imminent risk of destruction, with Shaktoolik ranking among the top four. Some villages, climate change experts predict, will be uninhabitable by 2050, their residents joining a flow of climate refugees around the globe, in Bolivia, China, Niger and other countries.

These endangered Alaskan communities face a choice. They could move to higher ground, a wrenching prospect that for a small village could cost as much as $200 million. Or they could stand their ground and hope to find money to fortify their buildings and shore up their coastline.

At least two villages farther up the western coast, Shishmaref and Kivalina, have voted to relocate when and if they can find a suitable site and the money to do so. A third, Newtok, in the soggy Yukon-Kuskokwim Delta farther south, has taken the first steps toward a move.

But, after years of meetings that led nowhere and pleas for government financing that remained unmet, Shaktoolik has decided it will "stay and defend," at least for the time being, the mayor, Eugene Asicksik, said.

"We are doing things on our own," he said.

The tiny Cessna carrying two visitors touches down lightly on the thin gravel strip that in Shaktoolik serves as an airport.

It is mid-September, and with the commercial fishing season over, the village is preparing for winter.

Moose meat simmers on the stove in the house of Matilda Hardy, president of the Native Village of Shaktoolik Council. Jean Mute, the pastor's wife, stoops to pick cranberries for preserves in a field just outside town.

By the river, a fisherman works on his boat, preparing it to hunt beluga whales in the shallow waters of the Norton Sound. In the evening, a boy outside the snack shop where children drink fruit slushies and munch on Kit-Kat bars proudly holds up a fat goose he shot in the day's hunting expedition.

The ocean is calm, but bad weather is already on people's minds.

"I'm wondering what our fall storms will bring," Ms. Hardy says. As of late November, there had been one high tide, but no severe storm.

In Shaktoolik, as in other villages around the state, residents say winter is arriving later than before and rushing prematurely into spring, a shift scientists tie to climate change. With rising ocean temperatures, the offshore ice and slush that normally buffer the village from storm surges and powerful ocean waves are decreasing. Last winter, for the first time elders here can remember, there was no offshore ice at all.

The battering delivered by the storms has eaten away at the land around the village, which occupies 1.1 square miles on a three-mile strip of land. According to one estimate, that strip is losing an average of 38,000 square feet — or almost an acre — a year. Flooding from the ocean and the swollen river waters has become so severe that the last big storm came close to turning Shaktoolik into an island.

"That was pretty scary," said Agnes Takak, the administrative assistant for the village's school. "It seemed like the waves would wash right over and cover us, but thankfully they didn't."

As Shaktoolik and other threatened villages have discovered, both staying and moving have their perils.

The process of relocation can take years or even decades. In the meantime, residents still need to send their children to school, go to the doctor when they are sick, have functioning water lines and fuel tanks and a safe place to go when a severe storm comes.

But few government agencies are willing to invest in maintaining villages that are menaced by erosion and flooding, especially when the communities are planning to pull up stakes and go elsewhere.

"It's a real Catch-22 situation," said Sally Cox, the state's coordinator for the native villages.

Even announcing the intention to relocate can scuttle a community's request for financing. Some years ago, when Shaktoolik indicated on a grant proposal that it was hoping to move, it lost funds for its clinic, said Isabel Jackson, the city clerk.

Shaktoolik's leaders have identified a potential relocation site 11 miles southeast, near the foothills. But some residents say they fear that their culture, dependent on fishing and hunting, will suffer if they move. And Edgar Jackson Sr., a former mayor, said that the government turned down applications for money to build a road that would serve both as a way to get building materials to their new home and as an evacuation route. Residents currently have no reliable way to escape quickly in an emergency.

"We called it an 'evacuation' road, a 'relocation' road," Mr. Jackson said. "The state and federal government didn't like those two words."

Shaktoolik — the name means "scattered things" in a native language — has been forced to move twice before in its history. The Eskimo tribes that traveled from the north into the region in the mid-1800s found an Eden of berry fields, tundra where moose and herds of caribou grazed and waters where salmon, seals and beluga flourished.

By the early 1900s, they had settled into a site six miles up the Shaktoolik River. But in the 1930s, the federal Bureau of Indian Affairs, responsible for providing educational services to Native Americans, built a two-room schoolhouse on the coastal sand spit, and the residents were compelled to move there if their children were to go to school.

The "old site," as village residents call it, was where many elders in Shaktoolik grew up; the skeletal remains of the buildings are still standing, a ghost town that sits three miles from the village.

But that location, chosen by the federal government, put Shaktoolik at the mercy of the fierce storms that barreled into the sound from the Aleutian Islands.

After a series of close calls in the 1960s — one severe storm destroyed boats and left the airport littered with driftwood, making it impossible for planes to land — another move seemed inevitable.

Two new sites were proposed, one on higher ground near the foot-hills, the other the spot the village now occupies.

At a series of three public meetings, the residents debated the choices.

Mr. Jackson, who was mayor at the time, recalled that he and his wife were in favor of moving to higher ground.

"That would have solved our problems," he said. "But majority ruled. We were short three votes."

When the fall storms come, they almost always come at night, the waves hurling giant driftwood logs onto the beach like toothpicks, the river rising, the wind shaking the windows of the houses that sit in two orderly rows along Shaktoolik's single road. Children who in summer play outside long after dark hunker down with their parents, listening to the CB radio announcements that serve as the village's central form of communication.

Big storms on Alaska's west coast are different from those that threaten Miami or New Orleans. They can carry the force of a Category 1 hurricane, but their diameter is five to 10 times greater, meaning that they affect a larger area and last longer, said Robert E. Jensen, research hydraulic engineer at the Army Corps of Engineers Research and Development Center.

"They're huge," he said.

Some residents here say that the storms are becoming more frequent and more intense, although scientists do not have data to confirm this. But there is no question that higher ocean temperatures have resulted in less offshore ice, allowing storm surges and waves to hit with greater force and bringing more flooding and erosion.

The loss of sea ice, said David Atkinson, a climate scientist at the University of Victoria in British Columbia, is "undeniably linked" to a warming climate, as is the rising level of the sea as a result of melting glaciers, the increased volume of water lending even more strength to the ocean's assault.

Fifty years ago, when the beach was a quarter of a mile away, the increasing violence of the ocean might not have bothered Shaktoolik's residents. But now the sea is almost at their doorsteps.

At one time, Ms. Hardy, the council president, could see the beach from her window.

Now she looks out instead on a berm, a mile-long, seven-foot-high mound of driftwood and gravel built by the village as a barrier against an angry ocean.

Two state engineers came up with the idea, but they ran out of money before they produced a design.

Mayor Asicksik decided to go ahead anyway. Local men hauled the gravel from the mouth of the river in old military trucks bought for $9,000 each and finished the project in less than four months.

Residents here are proud of the berm: It is a symbol of their determination to fix their own problems without help from the government.

But most also realize that the makeshift barricade is only a stop-gap; some question whether it will last even through one big storm.

"It hasn't been tested yet," Ms. Hardy said.

Shaktoolik faces other threats that will be difficult or impossible to ward off without assistance.

Erosion is threatening the village's fuel tanks, its airport and its drinking water supply, which is pumped from the Tagoomenik River. The boundary between river and sea has been so thinned by erosion in some spots that salt water from the ocean, normally a benign source of sustenance, briefly overtopped the bank and poured into the river during a recent storm.

The land continues to disintegrate. The Army Corps of Engineers assessment, while cautioning that its conclusions were based on limited data, estimated that the spit that Shaktoolik sits on could lose 45 acres by 2057, with rising water threatening fuel tanks, commercial buildings and the air strip.

But the most urgent challenge is keeping village residents safe in the event of a disaster.

Shaktoolik's current emergency plan calls for people to gather inside the school. But the school building, which sits on the ocean side of the road, is itself likely to be flooded and is not large enough to comfortably accommodate everyone, even if it stays dry.

Some families have said that in a severe storm they would flee up the Shaktoolik River. They keep their boats stocked with supplies. But the river, Mayor Asicksik and others said, would almost certainly be ice-filled and treacherous, and any attempt to escape would likely end in a search and rescue operation.

Even the airport is risky. Carven Scott, Alaska regional director for the National Weather Service, who recently visited Shaktoolik, said that after Hurricane Irene hit the East Coast in 2011, the service conducted an assessment for future storms and concluded that the several million people who lived in vulnerable areas of the Northeast could be evacuated in about 12 hours.

A similar evacuation in Shaktoolik, Mr. Scott said, might take five days.

With bad weather conditions and low light, "the chances are we could not get a sizable aircraft in there far enough in advance to evacuate," he said. "You'd have to take people out in groups of 10 or less."

Yet if it is to stay put, the village must find a way to prevent loss of life, if not the loss of property.

"They do not want to move and I have to accept that," said David Williams, a project engineer for the Alaska division of the Corps of Engineers and a member of an interagency group that is helping endangered villages plan for the future.

"But if they want to live here," Mr. Williams said, "they have to have a way to get out of Dodge when getting out is required."

Kirby Sookiayak, the village's community coordinator, sits in his office and ticks off the community's wish list: an evacuation road; improvements to the water system and the fuel tank farm; increased fortification of the berm; floodlights and lighted buoys for the river; a new health clinic; a fortified shelter for residents in a storm.

The estimated price tag for these improvements? Well over $100 million, according to Shaktoolik's recently completed strategic management plan. And while state and federal agencies will finance some routine work, it will not even be close to what is needed.

No one knows where the additional money will come from. Despite years of government reports calling for action, sporadic bursts of financing and a visit to the region by President Obama last year, the hundreds of millions of dollars it would take for Alaska's threatened villages to stay where they are — or to move elsewhere — have not materialized.

In Kivalina and Shishmaref, the Corps of Engineers was able to build sturdy rock revetments to armor the villages, authorized by Congress in 2005 to do so at federal expense. But the law was rescinded four years later, and the corps can do nothing more without the villages coming up with matching funds of their own.

The state of Alaska — which in the past provided some funds to Newtok, allowing the Yupik community to begin its move across the river to safety — is in a fiscal crisis, its economic health tied to oil revenues. And a federal lawsuit filed by one village against oil and coal companies, seeking relocation money as compensation for their air pollution, went nowhere.

Shaktoolik is scheduled to receive $1 million from the Denali Commission, an independent federal agency created in 1998 to help provide services to rural Alaskan communities. But the money will not go far: some will help pay for a new design to fortify the berm, while the rest is intended to help protect the village's fuel tank storage.

Perhaps the largest potential contribution is the $400 million allocated for relocating threatened villages in the Obama administration's proposed 2017 budget. But with a new administration, the fate of that allocation is at best uncertain.

"I wish they'd come and spend one day in one of our storms," Axel Jackson, who sits on the village council, said of politicians in Washington. The federal government spends billions on wars in foreign countries, he said. "But they still treat us like we're a third world country."

PRODUCED BY CRAIG ALLEN, GRAY BELTRAN, HANNAH FAIRFIELD, DAVID FURST, TAIGE JENSEN, MEAGHAN LOORAM AND JEREMY WHITE.

# As Climate Changes, Southern States Will Suffer More Than Others

BY BRAD PLUMER AND NADJA POPOVICH  |  JUNE 29, 2017

AS THE UNITED STATES confronts global warming in the decades ahead, not all states will suffer equally. Maine may benefit from milder winters. Florida, by contrast, could face major losses, as deadly heat waves flare up in the summer and rising sea levels eat away at valuable coastal properties.

In a new study in the journal Science, researchers analyzed the economic harm that climate change could inflict on the United States in the coming century. They found that the impacts could prove highly unequal: states in the Northeast and West would fare relatively well, while parts of the Midwest and Southeast would be especially hard hit.

In all, the researchers estimate that the nation could face damages worth 0.7 percent of gross domestic product per year by the 2080s for every 1 degree Fahrenheit rise in global temperature. But that overall number obscures wide variations: The worst-hit counties — mainly in states that already have warm climates, like Arizona or Texas — could see losses worth 10 to 20 percent of G.D.P. or more if emissions continue to rise unchecked.

"The reason for that is fairly well understood: A rise in temperatures is a lot more damaging if you're living in a place that's already hot," said Solomon Hsiang, a professor of public policy at the University of California, Berkeley, and a lead author of the study.

"You see a similar pattern internationally, where countries in the tropics are more heavily impacted by climate change," he said. "But this is the first study to show that same pattern of inequality in the United States."

The greatest economic impact would come from a projected increase in heat wave deaths as temperatures soared, which is why states like Alabama and Georgia would face higher risks while the cooler Northeast would not. If communities do not take preventative measures, the projected increase in heat-related deaths by the end of this century would be roughly equivalent to the number of Americans killed annually in auto accidents.

Higher temperatures could also lead to steep increases in energy costs in parts of the country, as utilities may need to overbuild their grids to compensate for heavier air-conditioning use in hot months. Labor productivity in many regions is projected to suffer, especially for outdoor workers in sweltering summer heat. And higher sea levels along the coasts would make flooding from future hurricanes far more destructive.

The authors avoided delving into politics, but they warned that "climate change tends to increase pre-existing inequality." Some of the poorest regions of the country could see the largest economic losses, particularly in the Southeast. That pattern would hold even if the world's nations cut emissions drastically, though the overall economic losses would be considerably lower.

Predicting the costs of climate change is a fraught task, one that has bedeviled researchers for years. They have to grapple with uncertainty involving population growth, future levels of greenhouse-gas emissions, the effect of those emissions on the Earth's climate and the economic damage higher temperatures may cause.

Previous economic models have been relatively crude, focusing on broad global impacts. The new study, led by the Climate Impact Lab, a group of scientists, economists and computational experts, took advantage of a wealth of recent research on how high temperatures can cripple the economy. And the researchers harnessed advances in computing to scale global climate models down to individual counties in the United States.

"Past models had only looked at the United States as a single region," said Robert E. Kopp, a climate scientist at Rutgers and a lead author of the study. "They missed this entire story of how climate change would create this large transfer of wealth between states."

There are still limitations to the study. It relies heavily on research showing how hot weather has caused economic losses in the past. But society and technology will change a lot over the next 80 years, and people may find novel ways to adapt to steadily rising temperatures, said Robert S. Pindyck, an economist at the Massachusetts Institute of Technology who was not involved with this study.

Urban planners could set up cooling centers during heat waves to help vulnerable people who lack air-conditioning, as France did after a heat wave killed 14,802 people in 2003. Farmers may adopt new crop varieties or shift planting patterns to cope with the rise in scorching heat.

Notably, the model also does not account for the effects of future migration within the United States. If Arizona becomes unbearable because of rising temperatures, more people may decide to move to states like Oregon or Montana, which would largely escape intolerable heat waves and could even see an increase in agricultural production. Such migration could reduce the country's overall economic losses, said Matthew E. Kahn, an economist at the University of Southern California.

Other outside experts praised the study, but cautioned that it may have underestimated certain kinds of damages. Economic losses on the coasts could be far higher if ice sheets in Antarctica and Greenland disintegrate faster than expected. And climate change could bring other calamities that are harder to tally, such as the loss of valuable ecosystems like Florida's coral reefs, or increased flows of refugees from other countries facing their own climate challenges.

The study also does not factor in how reduced labor productivity could compound over time, leading to slower rates of economic growth, said Frances C. Moore, a climate expert at the University of California, Davis.

The researchers at the lab plan to expand their model to include more possible impacts and provide a detailed view of what individual counties can expect, so policymakers can begin to prepare far in advance.

"That's the hope, that this research can help prevent many of these outcomes," said Trevor Houser, a co-author of the paper who helps direct the Climate Impact Lab. "If cities take action to prevent heat wave deaths by building cooling centers, then costs would be lower than we project. But I wouldn't see that as a failure of prediction — that's a policy success."

# Climate Change in My Backyard

**OPINION** | **BY LEAH C. STOKES** | **JAN. 11, 2018**

SANTA BARBARA, CALIF. — On Tuesday morning, half an inch of water fell in nearby Montecito — half an inch in five minutes. Even in the best of conditions, this pace could cause flooding. But it wasn't the best of conditions. Last month, we endured the largest wildfire in California history.

For two and a half weeks straight, the fire burned closer every day. Air quality turned unhealthy and forced schools to close. Businesses had to shut their doors during the peak holiday season. The local economy was decimated. I moved out of my home for weeks, as did many others. But at least I had a home to return to. Hundreds of others lost theirs. Thousands more lost their livelihoods. As a climate policy researcher, I was seeing the consequences of climate inaction in my own backyard.

MARK PERNICE

Life was just beginning to get back to normal when the rains came this week, hard and fast. The scorched land could not absorb the water, and so the mudslides began.

Many residents, exhausted from weeks of displacement, were at home that night despite evacuation warnings. The forecast called for heavy rains, and the county was persistent in its preparation for mudslides and flooding. But the rain's intensity was extreme. Rain was not supposed to fall this fast, not in our memory. No one thought it would be so bad.

Houses were ripped from their foundations. City streets were unrecognizable. Helicopters flew back and forth in a near continuous line for days, hoisting people from roofs. The names of the missing and the dead swelled.

We say the extreme rain caused this disaster. We say it was the fire. And we say that multiple years of drought didn't help. But what caused the rain, the fire and the drought?

There is a clear climate signature in the disaster in Santa Barbara. We know that climate change is making California's extreme rainfall events more frequent. We know it's worsening our fires. We know that it contributed substantially to the latest drought.

There are simpler stories we could tell. Stories with more proximate causes: Those people bought in dangerous places. Those people should have left their homes. Those people are somehow to blame. These events are normal. These things just happen there.

But these simple stories mask a larger truth. How many times do we need to hear adjectives in their superlative form before we spot a pattern: largest, rainiest, driest, deadliest? Records, by their nature, are not meant to be set annually. And yet that's what is happening. The costliest year for natural disasters in the United States was 2017. One of the longest and most severe droughts in California history concluded for most parts of the state in 2017. The five warmest years on record have all occurred since 2006, with 2017 expected to be one of the warmest yet again.

I have researched climate change policy for over a decade now. For a long time, we assumed that climate policy was stalled because it was a problem for the future. Or it would affect other people. Poorer people. Animals. Ecosystems. We assumed those parts of the world were separate from us. That we were somehow insulated. I didn't expect to see it in my own backyard so soon.

Climate change devastated ecosystems, species and neighborhoods in Houston and much of struggling Puerto Rico last year. Now climate change has ravaged one of the wealthiest ZIP codes in the country. We know now that even the richest among us is not insulated.

These extreme events are getting worse. But when I read the news after each fresh disaster, I rarely see a mention of climate change. Whether it's coverage of a fire in my backyard or a powerful hurricane in the Caribbean, this bigger story is usually missing. To say that it is too soon to talk about the causes of a crisis is wrongheaded. We must connect the dots.

Climate change helped cost my friends' businesses' revenue. Climate change helped put my community in chaos for weeks. Climate change paved the way for lost lives next door. If climate victims here and across the globe understood that carbon emissions from burning fossil fuels played a role in their losses, perhaps they would rise up to demand policy changes.

We know this could happen because research from the political scientist Regina Bateson, now a congressional candidate in California, shows that being a crime victim can spur people into activism. Perhaps some of the people affected by the fires in California, the hurricanes in Puerto Rico and Texas, and the drought in the Dakotas will be similarly motivated. Maybe some of these climate change victims will become the climate policy champions we sorely need.

It is never too soon after one of these disasters to speak truth about climate change's role. If anything, it is too late. If we do not name the problem, we cannot hope to solve it. For my community, as much as yours, I hope we will.

**LEAH C. STOKES** IS AN ASSISTANT PROFESSOR OF POLITICAL SCIENCE AT THE UNIVERSITY OF CALIFORNIA, SANTA BARBARA.

# Drought and War Heighten Threat of Not Just 1 Famine, but 4

BY JEFFREY GETTLEMAN | MARCH 27, 2017

BAIDOA, SOMALIA — First the trees dried up and cracked apart.

Then the goats keeled over.

Then the water in the village well began to disappear, turning cloudy, then red, then slime-green, but the villagers kept drinking it. That was all they had.

Now on a hot, flat, stony plateau outside Baidoa, thousands of people pack into destitute camps, many clutching their stomachs, some defecating in the open, others already dead from a cholera epidemic.

"Even if you can get food, there is no water," said one mother, Sangabo Moalin, who held her head with a left hand as thin as a leaf and spoke of her body "burning."

TYLER HICKS/THE NEW YORK TIMES

A dusty dirt road winds across a dry, stark landscape in Baidoa, Somalia.

Another famine is about to tighten its grip on Somalia. And it's not the only crisis that aid agencies are scrambling to address. For the first time since anyone can remember, there is a very real possibility of four famines — in Somalia, South Sudan, Nigeria and Yemen — breaking out at once, endangering more than 20 million lives.

International aid officials say they are facing one of the biggest humanitarian disasters since World War II. And they are determined not to repeat the mistakes of the past.

One powerful lesson from the last famine in Somalia, just six years ago, was that famines were not simply about food. They are about something even more elemental: water.

Once again, a lack of clean water and proper hygiene is setting off an outbreak of killer diseases in displaced persons camps. So the race is on to dig more latrines, get swimming-pool quantities of clean water into the camps, and pass out more soap, more water-treatment tablets and more plastic buckets — decidedly low-tech supplies that could save many lives.

TYLER HICKS/THE NEW YORK TIMES

An elderly woman displaced by the drought in Somalia walking between makeshift tents that are now home to the desperate at a camp in Baidoa.

"We underestimated the role of water and its contribution to mortality in the last famine," said Ann Thomas, a water, sanitation and hygiene specialist for Unicef. "It gets overshadowed by the food."

The famines are coming as a drought sweeps across Africa and several different wars seal off extremely needy areas. United Nations officials say they need a huge infusion of cash to respond. So far, they are not just millions of dollars short, but billions.

At the same time, President Trump is urging Congress to cut foreign aid and assistance to the United Nations, which aid officials fear could multiply the deaths. The United States traditionally provides more disaster relief than anyone else.

"The international humanitarian system is at its breaking point," said Dominic MacSorley, chief executive of Concern Worldwide, a large private aid group.

Aid officials say all the needed food and water exist on this planet in abundance — even within these hard-hit countries. But armed conflict

TYLER HICKS/THE NEW YORK TIMES

Mothers tending to their children at a cholera treatment center. A lack of clean water triggered an outbreak of the disease.

that is often created by personal rivalries between a few men turns life upside down for millions, destroying markets and making the price of necessities go berserk.

In some areas of central Somalia, a 20-liter jerry can of water, about five and a quarter gallons, used to cost 4 cents. In recent weeks, that price has shot up to 42 cents. That may not sound like a lot. But when you make less than a dollar a day and your flock of animals — your family's pride and wealth — has been reduced to a stack of bleached bones and your farm to dust, you may not have 42 cents.

"There is no such thing as free water," said Isaac Nur Abdi, a nomad, who sat in the dusky gloom of a cholera treatment center in Baidoa this month. He fanned his elderly mother, whose cavernous eye sockets and protruding cheekbones bore the telltale signature of famine.

Scenes like this are unfolding across the region. In Yemen, relentless aerial bombings by Saudi Arabia and a trade blockade have mutilated the economy, sending food prices spiraling and pushing hundreds of thousands of children to the brink of starvation.

In northeastern Nigeria, thousands of displaced people have become sick from diseases spread by dirty water and poor hygiene as the battle grinds on between Islamist militants and the Nigerian military, which, when it comes to protecting the vulnerable, does not have the most stellar record. The Nigerian Air Force bombed a displaced persons camp in January, killing scores, saying it was an accident.

In South Sudan, both rebel forces and government soldiers are intentionally blocking emergency food and hijacking food trucks, aid officials say. On Saturday, six aid workers were killed, complicating relief efforts even further. Entire communities are marooned in malarial swamps trying to survive off barely chewable lotus plants and worm-infested swamp water.

While the other countries are technically on the brink of famine, the United Nations has already declared parts of South Sudan a famine zone.

An ailing and barely conscious man being rushed to a cholera treatment center.

Scientists have been saying for years that climate change will increase the frequency of droughts. The hardest-hit countries, though, produce almost none of the carbon emissions that are widely believed to cause climate change.

South Sudan and Somalia, for instance, have relatively few vehicles and almost no industry. But their fields are drying up and their pastureland is vanishing, scientists say, partly because of the global effects of pollution. People in these countries suffer from other people's driving, other people's manufacturing and other people's attachment to things like flat-screen TVs and iPads that most Somalis and South Sudanese will touch only in their dreams.

It's not simple to get food and clean water into these areas where everything is dried out, yellow and dead.

Baidoa itself is controlled by Somalia's fledging government and African Union troops. But just a few miles outside the town, it is

Shabab country, belonging to the Shabab militant Islamist group that has banned Western aid agencies.

"The fact that people are dying near Baidoa and we can't get there, it makes me crazy," said Patrick Laurent, a water and sanitation coordinator hired by Unicef in Somalia.

After Somalia's last famine, the multibillion-dollar aid industry thought it had come up with an answer to prevent the next one: resilience. It was the new buzzword in aid circles, bandied about at workshops and among high-powered officials.

Aid officials defined resilience as the ability to adapt to sudden environmental or political shocks. Resilience programs included livestock insurance and better water management, especially in Africa.

Some aid officials never liked this term, saying it seemed patronizing, as if Africans were built to suffer. Still, the resilience subindustry roared on.

But just as many of the new resilience programs were being funded, these latest crises hit, one after the other.

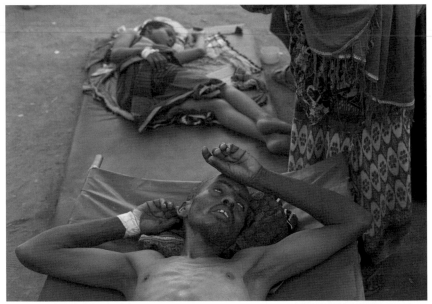

TYLER HICKS/THE NEW YORK TIMES

An ailing man on a cot, and a boy on the ground. There are not enough beds and cots for all the patients.

"The environment didn't give time for these resilience efforts to bear fruit," Mr. Laurent said.

Ms. Thomas, the Unicef water and hygiene specialist, said that during Somalia's last famine, the deadliest areas were not the empty deserts where there was little food but the displaced-persons camps near urban areas where, comparatively speaking, there was plenty of food.

The reason was that the crowded camps became hotbeds of communicable diseases like cholera, a bacterial infection that can lead to very painful intestinal cramps, diarrhea and fatal dehydration. Cholera is often caused by dirty water and spread by exposure to contaminated feces through fingers, food and flies.

Malnutrition certainly played its part; famine victims, especially children, were compromised by a lack of nutrients. They arrived in the camps from wasted areas of the interior with their immune systems already shot.

But in the end it was poor hygiene and dirty water, Ms. Thomas said, that tugged many down.

If rivers and other relatively clean water sources start drying up, as they are right now in Somalia, this sets off an interlocking cycle of death. People start to get sick at their stomachs from the slimy or cloudy water they are forced to drink. They start fleeing their villages, hoping to get help in the towns.

Camps form. But the camps do not have enough water either, and it is hard to find a latrine or enough water for people to wash their hands. Shockingly fast, the camps become disease factories.

Water, of course, is less negotiable than food. A human being can survive weeks with nothing to eat. Five days without water means death.

Different strategies are being emphasized this time around to parry the famine. One is simply giving out cash.

United Nations agencies and private aid groups in Somalia are scaling up efforts to dole out money through a new electronic card system and by mobile phone. This allows poor people to get a monthly allowance and shop for staples like fresh vegetables, powdered milk,

A hospital employee spraying disinfectant in a tent at a cholera treatment center. The crowded camps can become hotbeds of communicable diseases.

pasta, dates, sugar, salt and camel meat. Cash payments are often better for the local economy than importing sacks of food, and the people get help fast.

Many more Africans may soon need it. Sweltering days and poor rains so far this year have left Burundi, Kenya, Rwanda, Uganda, Ethiopia and Tanzania parched and on the edge of a major food crisis.

At the cholera treatment center in Baidoa, which logged in more than 30 cases on a recent day, many people had little inkling of what caused cholera.

When Mr. Abdi, whose mother was nearly dead from the disease, was asked what had made his mother sick, he said the cause was simple.

It was the hot season.

# A Lifetime in Peru's Glaciers, Slowly Melting Away

BY NICHOLAS CASEY | JAN. 26, 2018

HUARAZ, PERU — At 50, Americo González Caldua has lived a life that coincided with the retreat of the glaciers of the high Andes. With each passing year, as the cold mountain temperatures rise, the ice moves uphill another 20 yards.

In the dry season, when the storms break and the research season begins, Mr. González heads to the icy heights of the nearby peaks with survey prisms and markers. He brings heavy drilling augers that bore core samples deep below the surface of the glaciers and reveal a picture of the atmosphere from a century ago.

He knows the ice sheet as well as anyone. Yet, Mr. González is neither a mountaineer nor a scientist: He's the man most often found trailing behind them, carrying their equipment.

Mount Everest has the Sherpas. The Cordillera Blanca, a snowy mountain range in northern Peru, has the ayudantes de campo, or field helpers, in Spanish. They are the mountain men, mainly indigenous, who have watched a huge expanse of ice that was known to them for centuries shrink drastically in the space of one generation.

"Before, we saw our glaciers as beautiful, our mountain range covered in a white sheet that was stunning," Mr. González said on a recent day at a small mountain-climber's hostel near the base of an 18,000-foot peak. "But today, we don't see that anymore on our glacier, which we're losing more of every day. Instead of white, we are seeing stone."

Of all the glaciers in retreat throughout the world, those in this part of South America are the most likely to disappear first. Scientists call them the tropical glaciers, ice caps found in places as warm as Ecuador and Indonesia, where high mountain peaks have shielded them for thousands of years from the heat of the jungle below.

Yet now, even these high perches have become precarious. Climate scientists say the ice cap here has been reduced by nearly a quarter in the past 40 years because of rising temperatures. With the rate of melting increasing each year, some scientists predict that within 50 years many of the peaks here will no longer have glaciers.

"It's not Antarctica, where you have a rupture of a mile and everyone notices," said Justiniano Alejo Cochachin, a glaciologist who works for the Peruvian government. "It's 19 meters a year; it is bit by bit."

On his many journeys, Mr. González has spent decades looking over the shoulders of scientists like Mr. Cochachin, shaping his own intimate view of a landscape altered by climate change.

He watched the expanding rocky fields around the Pastoruri Glacier, where the melting ice uncovered fossils that had not seen daylight in ages, including those of ferns and other plants. He has seen rivers turn red as other glaciers melted and exposed heavy metals that poison the water downstream.

At current melt rates, the Gueshgue glacier and others in the Cordillera Blanca mountain range of Peru could disappear within 50 years, glaciologists say.

"If there is no water, there is no life," Mr. González said.

His work begins early, well before sunrise, when he packs crampons used to walk atop the glaciers, large boring drills and topographical instruments, helmets, gloves and the gear to build a shelter, all in a backpack nearly as large as he is.

The food often goes on a mule — provided the mule can make the climb. If not, Mr. González carries that, too, on several trips in and out of the camp over the course of several days.

Mr. González said the path on a recent climb to a glacier called Yanamarey would not be so taxing, by his standards — a round-trip journey of 10 hours. And so we headed out one morning with Rolando Cruz, a researcher in the nearby town of Huaraz who came to take some measurements at the base of the glacier.

The long hours up are often quiet ones, where Mr. González searches for what he calls the "perfect route" through the unmarked boggy landscape of mist and fog where jagged peaks rise up on either side and hawks soar above. Vast plains stretch for miles, former lake beds from the ice age, where cows graze.

"The cows weren't here before," noted Mr. González, saying they now graze at higher altitudes than before, as they follow the grasses as the temperatures have warmed.

The route was one that Mr. González has crossed countless times over the decades, since he first visited the Yanamarey glacier in the early 1990s. His descriptions of it from that time vary. At times he evokes a building — it had "blue walls," he said. Sometimes he spoke of the glacier's "beautiful long tongue," and it sounded more like an animal.

"Yes, it is alive," he said, describing the glacier's slow movement below his feet.

In the 1990s, the hikes could be an escape from the conflicts taking place below, when the Shining Path, the Maoist rebel group that terrorized Peru for decades, attacked politicians in Huaraz and planted three car bombs. Despite the unrest, American researchers would

Americo González Caldua, right, using a heavy drilling auger that bores core samples deep below the surface of the glaciers to reveal a picture of the atmosphere from a century ago.

come each year, and Mr. González would lead them up as the ice sheet continued to melt.

"When you go out into the field, your mind clears," he said.

It was the sound of the cracking, heard on nearly every ice sheet the scientists came to study, that bothered him most. "Tac," he said, "like a huge sound." And every year he came, Yanamarey was farther away than it had been the last time.

Our climb continued. The landscape turned into a rocky stretch of boulders. Then the glacier came into view.

It looked very different that day from the place Mr. González had described. The ice sheet, having once spilled into the lake below it, had retreated halfway up a rocky mountainside, a small spit peeking behind the rocks. There were no "blue walls," no "tongue," just a thin coat of ice over a bare rocky stretch.

"It looks gray, like the color of lead," Mr. González said several times.

Mr. Cruz climbed up, took his measurements in the distance and returned some time later. The two men looked at each other with the same resigned glance, then headed back down the hill.

At his age, Mr. González knows these journeys will not continue forever. His knees have begun to give out, particularly as he walks downhill with large amounts of gear. "You don't have the same strength," he said.

Mr. González looked over at his son Álvaro, an 18-year-old who had joined us that afternoon back at the hostel in Huaraz. The boy told me he would soon study climate science in college, inspired by his father who had taken him to see the ice sheet for the first time some years ago.

Who had shown Mr. González the glaciers first? It was his mother, he said, on a chilly day when the two were looking out at the peaks from a nearby farm.

"You could see those white glaciers in the distance," he said. "And our mother pointed to them and said in her language 'raju,' which is the Quechua word, which means ice."

Back then, the ice seemed as permanent as the mountains themselves.

"No, I never imagined this," said Mr. González, describing the ice today. "As a child, you can never picture the things which might happen."

**ANDREA ZARATE CONTRIBUTED REPORTING.**

# Floods Leave Paris
# Contemplating a Wetter Future

BY ELIAN PELTIER AND ELOISE STARK | JAN. 26, 2018

PARIS — Must France simply get used to flooding?

The Seine River overflowed its banks again in Paris and several nearby cities this week, a mere 18 months after reaching its highest level since 1982.

Thirteen of France's 96 administrative departments had flood alerts as of Friday, in what the monitoring body Météo-France says is the country's wettest winter since 1959.

Some experts suggest climate change is likely to make such events more frequent. And an international body chose this week to publish a study arguing that Paris and the rest of the Seine basin needed greater protection against the risk of a catastrophic flood.

"All we can do is put up scaffolding to make a pontoon, and hope that the water doesn't come up much higher," Diane Bourlier, a 63-year-old who lives on a houseboat in Paris, said as she looked anxiously out at the rising river.

Ms. Bourlier was among the lucky ones: As of Thursday night, 400 people had been evacuated from homes in the Paris region, and a thousand faced power cuts, according to the police prefecture. Rivers have swelled across the country, forcing evacuations and the closing of roads and infrastructure.

In Paris, where the Seine rose above 18 feet on Friday, river traffic has been interrupted and roads along the river banks remained closed. A central portion of the RER C train line has been shut until the end of the month, and the government activated a plan that could let it relocate work from some ministries if the situation worsens.

Public authorities said they expected the Seine to crest on Sunday at up to six meters, or about 19.6 feet. In the floods of June 2016, which killed four people in France, it peaked at 20 feet.

During those floods, several monuments had to be closed, including the Louvre Museum, where artworks had to be evacuated. All museums remained open this week, although the Louvre shut the lower level of its department of Islamic Arts. The city authorities have also called on people to stay away from the river banks.

Although some experts said it was hard to determine whether global warming was behind the current flood, others warned that a worrying pattern was emerging.

"Because of climate change, we can expect floods in the Seine basin to be at least as frequent as they are right now," said Florence Habets, a senior researcher at the C.N.R.S., France's national center for scientific research. "No matter what we say, the more we reduce our greenhouse gas emissions, the more we reduce our impact on droughts and floods."

The mayor of Paris, Anne Hidalgo, a left-wing politician who has been at the forefront of the fight against climate change, was also quick to mention long-term challenges.

"Beyond the emergency, this flooding phenomenon, which is more and more recurrent in Paris, reminds us how important it is for our city to adapt to climate change," she said in a tweet.

Deputy Mayor Colombe Brossel said in a phone interview that although the situation was serious, the floods would have few concrete consequences in Paris.

They were certainly far less severe than some the city endured during the past century. In 1910, the Seine rose above 28 feet, giving Paris "the aspect of a beleaguered place," according to a New York Times report of the time.

Although local officials said they were now prepared to face similar conditions, experts from the Organization for Economic Cooperation and Development estimated that such a catastrophe could affect five million people and cost up to 30 billion euros, or about $37 billion.

In a study published on Tuesday, they noted that although Paris had implemented further flood prevention policies since 2014, the authorities' efforts remained limited compared to the risks the city faced.

"Examples from the reconstruction of a resilient New Orleans after Hurricane Katrina, or New York after Sandy, could inspire Paris to build up its own resilience before disaster hits," they wrote.

Heavy rains also flooded parts of eastern and northwestern France this week, blocking roads and inundating households that had already been affected by the torrential rains of 2016.

One of the most affected areas was the town of Villeneuve-St.-Georges, 10 miles south of Paris, where the military had to help residents evacuate their homes and propel themselves on dinghies through streets flooded with brownish water and waste.

"For some people, this is the second time in 18 months that they have been victims of floods," Alexandre Boyer, a local councilman, said. "It's beginning to get a little too much."

**TANGUY GARREL-JAFFRELOT CONTRIBUTED REPORTING.**

# Warming, Water Crisis, Then Unrest: How Iran Fits an Alarming Pattern

BY SOMINI SENGUPTA | JAN. 18, 2018

UNITED NATIONS — Nigeria. Syria. Somalia. And now Iran.

In each country, in different ways, a water crisis has triggered some combination of civil unrest, mass migration, insurgency or even full-scale war.

In the era of climate change, their experiences hold lessons for a great many other countries. The World Resources Institute warned this month of the rise of water stress globally, "with 33 countries projected to face extremely high stress in 2040."

A water shortage can spark street protests: Access to water has been a common source of unrest in India. It can be exploited by terrorist groups: The Shabab has sought to take advantage of the most vulnerable drought-stricken communities in Somalia. Water shortages can prompt an exodus from the countryside to crowded cities: Across the arid Sahel, young men unable to live off the land are on the move. And it can feed into insurgencies: Boko Haram stepped into this breach in Nigeria, Chad and Niger.

Iran is the latest example of a country where a water crisis, long in the making, has fed popular discontent. That is particularly true in small towns and cities in what is already one of the most parched regions of the world. Farms turned barren, lakes became dust bowls. Millions moved to provincial towns and cities, and joblessness led to mounting discontent among the young. Then came a crippling drought, lasting roughly 14 years.

In short, a water crisis — whether caused by nature, human mismanagement, or both — can be an early warning signal of trouble ahead. A panel of retired United States military officials warned in December that water stress, which they defined as a shortage of fresh water, would emerge as "a growing factor in the world's hot spots and conflict areas."

"With escalating global population and the impact of a changing climate, we see the challenges of water stress rising with time," the retired officials concluded in the report by CNA, a research organization based in Arlington, Virginia.

Climate change is projected to make Iran hotter and drier. A former Iranian agriculture minister, Issa Kalantari, once famously said that water scarcity, if left unchecked, would make Iran so harsh that 50 million Iranians would leave the country altogether.

### IS WATER THE REASON FOR THE LATEST UNREST IN IRAN?

Not entirely. Water alone doesn't explain the outbreak of protests that began in early January and spread swiftly across the country. But as David Michel, an analyst at the Stimson Center put it, the lack of water — whether it's dry taps in the city, or dry wells in the countryside, or dust storms rising from a shrinking Lake Urmia — is one of the most common, most visible markers of the government's failure to deliver basic services.

"Water is not going to bring down the government," he said. "But it's a component — in some towns, a significant component — of grievances and frustrations."

Managing water, he said, is the government's "most important policy challenge."

### HOW DID IT GET THIS BAD?

Like many countries, from India to Syria, Iran after the 1979 revolution set out to be self-sufficient in food. It wasn't a bad goal, in and of itself. But as the Iranian water expert Kaveh Madani points out, it meant that the government encouraged farmers to plant thirsty crops like wheat throughout the country. The government went further by offering farmers cheap electricity and favorable prices for their wheat — effectively a generous two-part subsidy that served as an incentive to plant more and more wheat and extract more and more groundwater.

The result: "25 percent of the total water that is withdrawn from aquifers, rivers and lakes exceeds the amount that can be replenished" by nature, according to Claudia Sadoff, a water specialist who prepared a report for the World Bank on Iran's water crisis.

Iran's groundwater depletion rate is today among the fastest in the world, so much so that by Mr. Michel's calculations, 12 of the country's 31 provinces "will entirely exhaust their aquifers within the next 50 years." In parts of the country, the groundwater loss is causing the land to sink.

Water is a handy political tool, and to curry favor with their rural base, Iran's leaders — and particularly the Islamic Revolutionary Guards Corps — dammed rivers across the country to divert water to key areas. As a result, many of Iran's lakes have shrunk. That includes Lake Urmia, once the region's largest saltwater lake, which has diminished in size by nearly 90 percent since the early 1970s.

## DOES CLIMATE CHANGE PLAY A ROLE?

According to the government, Iran expects a 25 percent decline in surface water runoff — rainfall and snow melt — by 2030. In the region as a whole, summers are predicted to get hotter, by two to three degrees Celsius at current rates of warming, according to the Intergovernmental Panel on Climate Change. Rains are projected to decline by 10 percent.

A 2015 study by two scientists at the Massachusetts Institute of Technology predicted that, at current rates of warming, "many major cities in the region could exceed a tipping point for human survival."

For the leaders of water-stressed countries, the most sobering lesson comes from nearby Syria. Its drought, stretching from 2006 to 2009, prompted a mass migration from country to city and then unemployment among the young. Frustrations built up. And in 2011, street protests broke out, only to be crushed by the government of Bashar al-Assad. It piled on to long-simmering frustrations of Syrians under Mr. Assad's authoritarian rule. A civil war erupted, reshaping the Middle East.

Water, said Julia McQuaid, the deputy director of CNA, doesn't lead straight to conflict. "It can be a catalyst," she said. "It can be a thing that breaks the system."

# CHAPTER 3

# Forced Migration

Climate change causes conditions that drive people from their homes, forcing them to seek safer or more sustainable places to live. Due to rising sea levels, water scarcity and the inability to grow enough food, climate refugees across the world are growing in numbers. Even so, there are still those who wonder if climate change is a real phenomenon, while others consider how a warmer planet is driving human migration.

## Climate Change Claims a Lake, and an Identity

BY NICHOLAS CASEY | JULY 7, 2016

LLAPALLAPANI, BOLIVIA — The water receded and the fish died. They surfaced by the tens of thousands, belly-up, and the stench drifted in the air for weeks.

The birds that had fed on the fish had little choice but to abandon Lake Poopó, once Bolivia's second-largest but now just a dry, salty expanse. Many of the Uru-Murato people, who had lived off its waters for generations, left as well, joining a new global march of refugees fleeing not war or persecution, but climate change.

"The lake was our mother and our father," said Adrián Quispe, one of five brothers who were working as fishermen and raising families here in Llapallapani. "Without this lake, where do we go?"

After surviving decades of water diversion and cyclical El Niño droughts in the Andes, Lake Poopó basically disappeared in December.

The ripple effects go beyond the loss of livelihood for the Quispes and hundreds of other fishing families, beyond the migration of people forced to leave homes that are no longer viable.

The vanishing of Lake Poopó threatens the very identity of the Uru-Murato people, the oldest indigenous group in the area. They adapted over generations to the conquests of the Inca and the Spanish, but seem unable to adjust to the abrupt upheaval climate change has caused.

Only 636 Uru-Murato are estimated to remain in Llapallapani and two nearby villages. Since the fish died off in 2014, scores have left to work in lead mines or salt flats up to 200 miles away; those who stayed behind scrape by as farmers or otherwise survive on what used to be the shore.

Emilio Huanaco, an indigenous judicial official, is down to his last bottles of flamingo fat, used for centuries to alleviate arthritis. He has never used medication for his aching knee.

Eva Choque, 33, sat next to her adobe home drying meat for the first time on a clothesline. She and her four children ate only fish before.

They and their neighbors were known to nearly everyone in the area as "the people of the lake." Some adopted the last name Mauricio after the mauri, which is what they called a fish that used to fill their nets. They worshiped St. Peter because he was a fisherman, ritually offering him fish each September at the water's edge, but that celebration ended when the fish died two years ago.

"This is a millenarian culture that has been here since the start," said Carol Rocha Grimaldi, a Bolivian anthropologist whose office shows a satellite picture of a full lake, a scene no longer visible in real life. "But can the people of the lake exist without the lake?"

It is hard to overstate how central fishing was to Uru life. When a New York Times photographer, Josh Haner, and I asked Mr. Quispe whether he had made his living as a fisherman, he gave us a strange look before answering, essentially, "What else is there?"

Men spent stretches as long as two weeks without returning to shore, wandering the lake to follow schools of karachi, a gray fish that looked like a sardine, or pejerrey, which had big scales and grew as long as Mr. Quispe's arm.

Some wives worked alongside their husbands, to pull the nets and do the cooking, making the boats a kind of home.

Fishing season began on the lake's edge with a ritual called the Remembering. The Quispe brothers were among about 40 Llapal-lapani men who would pass a long night chewing coca leaf and drinking liquor. Together, the group recited the names of Lake Poopó's landmarks and how to find them.

"That night, we would ask for a safe journey, that there would be little wind, that there wouldn't be so much rain," Mr. Quispe, 42, told us. "We remembered all night, and we chewed our coca."

In the morning, the men would paddle out above the underwater springs known as jansuris. They would toss sweets from the boat as a religious offering. Fishing season had begun.

We were talking on a cloudless morning with a breeze that might have been perfect for a boat ride in another time. Now, the wind only underscored how dry the landscape had become, as tumbleweeds rolled between the boats abandoned on the old lake bed.

Milton Pérez, an ecologist at Oruro Technical University, said scientists had known for decades that Lake Poopó, which sits at 12,140 feet with few sources of water, fit the profile of what he called a dying lake. But the prognosis was in centuries, not years.

"We accepted the lake was going to die someday," Mr. Pérez said. "Now wasn't its time."

Lake Poopó is one of several lakes worldwide that are vanishing because of human causes. California's Mono Lake and Salton Sea were both diminished by water diversions; lakes in Canada and Mongolia are jeopardized by rising temperatures.

Generations of Uru had watched the water recede and return in what had almost become a predictable cycle. In the 1990s, a dry spell hit that evaporated the lake into three small ponds and destroyed the fisheries for several years. But the lake eventually returned to its previous size.

The Uru passed down knowledge about living on and around the lake. Crowds of large black birds on the horizon were an easy sign that fish were congregated below. They counted three distinct winds that could help or hurt: one from the west, another from the east, and a kind of squall from the north called the saucarí, which can sink boats.

"It awakens from the north and it doesn't calm down," Mr. Quispe explained. " 'The saucarí is coming,' we'd say. 'We can't go into the water until it calms!' "

The lake offered algae called huirahuira, which seemed to relieve coughs. Flamingos were like a pharmacy: In addition to the pink fat used to relieve rheumatism, the feathers fought fevers when burned and inhaled.

The villagers would catch and kill the flamingos in April, when the birds lost their feathers and were rendered flightless. The Uru used mirrors to cast sunlight in the birds' eyes, making them fall asleep temporarily, easy prey.

"We took so many of these from the lake," said Mr. Huanaco, the judicial leader, pulling out a bright pink wing from the mud hut behind his home. The day seven years ago that he hunted the bird down, he had no idea it would be his last.

Mr. Pérez, the researcher, watched with alarm as several threatening trends developed, and began to understand that the lake could evaporate for good.

First, as quinoa became popular abroad, booming production of the grain diverted water upstream, lowering Lake Poopó's level. Second, mining sediment was quickly silting the lake from below.

And it was getting hotter. The temperature on the plateau had increased 0.9 degrees Celsius, or about 1.6 degrees Fahrenheit, from 1995 to 2005 alone, much faster than Bolivia's national average.

"We had the possibility that all these factors would hit with a synergy never seen before," Mr. Pérez said.

In the summer of 2014, a rotten smell hung in the air. The surface of the lake had fallen so low that when the saucarí wind hit from the north, the gusts kicked up too much silt for the fish to survive.

"It was enough to make you cry, seeing the fish swimming dizzy or dead," Gabino Cepeda, a 44-year-old fisherman who has turned to farming quinoa, told us. "But that was just the start. The flamingos are dead, the ducks are gone, everything else. We threw out our nets, there was nothing for us."

Mr. Quispe and his brothers met one last time on the edge of the dead lake to perform the Remembering. They paddled out as they always had, but returned the same day because there were no fish.

The eldest, Teófilo, turned to his brothers.

"There is no work," he said. "I will figure out how to make money. And I will tell you how."

The next week, he left Llapallapani to work in a coal mine an hour's drive away.

Pablo Flores, another Uru fisherman who left Llapallapani, starts a thankless workday before sunrise inside a mill on the edge of the world's largest salt flat, Bolivia's Salar de Uyuni. He takes blocks of unrefined salt, grinds them down into a pile as high as he is tall, and puts them into tiny bags, earning 25 cents for each full one.

Outside the mill, it is more arduous. In the vast salt flat near the town of Colchani, where two dozen Uru have resettled, day laborers head out with shovels in the backs of trucks. They gather the salt as the heat beats down on them from above and reflects up from the white expanse below.

"The Uru people aren't made for this," Mr. Flores, 57, said. "I'm not made for this. We can't do this kind of work."

In his village, Puñaka, Mr. Flores was a respected elder. He was once its mayor, and people who knew him from that life still call him by the Spanish honorific "don." As a fisherman, he was always his own boss.

But at the salt mine, he feels like just another hired hand to exploit.

"This is a feudal system," he said. "I can sincerely say this is a bad place."

Looking over the heap of salt, he remembered an old legend, about a flood that destroyed the world — except for the Uru, who escaped on their balsa rafts and hid on a hilltop when the water began to recede. Disasters were meant to take the form of deluge, not drought, he said.

Some Uru men have left alone, sending money back to relatives who remain on the lake. But others, like Mr. Flores, have taken their families into a new world that has already begun transforming life in ways large and small.

Fifteen Uru live in Machacamarca, a dusty town of several thousand that was once a stop along an old railroad line to the lake. María Flores Ignacio and her two teenage children moved this spring into a rented apartment, a first for Ms. Flores, whose adobe home in Llapallapani was handed down through generations.

"I am living in someone else's house," she said with a long sigh.

To pay the rent, Ms. Flores makes straw handicrafts that she sells to tourists in the state capital, Oruro, at a Saturday market. There are hats, baskets, bracelets, earrings and small boats like the ones the Uru used to navigate Lake Poopó.

Back in Llapallapani, Mr. Cepeda, the fisherman-turned-farmer, wants out, too. But he doesn't have the money.

When the fish died, Mr. Cepeda staked his hopes on quinoa, an ancient crop in the Andes that is now in vogue in Western countries.

He had inherited two hectares of land — about five acres — from his father. He did not quite know how to plant quinoa, but he scattered the seeds in the ground and hoped for the best.

Instead of luck, Mr. Cepeda got a devastating frost, which struck in March. Picking up a handful of the quinoa, he showed us his meager harvest, mostly pulverized. It blew away from his palm. Only a few grains remained that weren't dust.

The dry bed of Lake Poopó, near Llapallapani, Bolivia.

The lake had always been what mattered to the Uru, not the ground, Mr. Cepeda told us. But that was changing.

"We fight each other now," he said. "Here is my land. But someone says, 'Now you are encroaching.' And then someone else says, 'No, that's mine.'"

Francisco Flores, now 26, was a child when his grandparents told him about the day the Uru-Murato first tasted meat. It was the start of the 20th century, and the Uru had decided to leave the lake's floating islands made of reeds and mud and settle on its edge. They wore shoes for the first time and gave up dresses made of feathers or wool for Western clothes. After centuries of eating only fish, they tried lamb, Mr. Flores recalled being told, and "it was tough."

A century later, the Uru have hit a crossroads again, but one not of their choosing.

"I want to teach my child to fish," Mr. Flores said, stopping on the dirt road that leads to the cemetery filled with his forebears. "But I can't."

Another day, Mr. Haner and I followed Felix Condori, Llapalla-pani's mayor, to a city market to buy vegetables for the first time. He used to barter with the Aymara Indians, whose pastures lie north of the village, trading fish for potatoes and quinoa straight from his boat.

Now, instead, he counted out bills from a wad with his wife and mother, the three looking confused.

The mayor, who carries a cane used to punish village delinquents, reached out with his other hand to buy a bottle of Axe deodorant spray.

"This is all new to us," he said.

On the highway back from the salt flat with Adrián Quispe one day, we saw a flamingo perched on the side of the road, by a stream 100 miles from Lake Poopó. It made Mr. Quispe suddenly remember the soup his mother used to make.

We stopped the car, got out and walked into a watery landscape with snowcapped mountains in the distance and birds in front of us.

"This is what Lake Poopó once looked like," Mr. Quispe said.

An hour before, I had been in the salt mill with Mr. Flores, the former Puñaka mayor who moved to Colchani with his wife and two young children two years ago.

When he last took them back to Llapallapani for a visit, his 6-year-old daughter said something that gave him chills. She was staring at what used to be the lake, having never really known it not to be dry.

"Let's go to Colchani," she said. "Let's go home."

PRODUCED BY GRAY BELTRAN, HANNAH FAIRFIELD, ALEXANDRA GARCIA AND MEAGHAN LOORAM.

# Resettling China's 'Ecological Migrants'

BY EDWARD WONG | OCT. 25, 2016

MIAOMIAO LAKE VILLAGE, CHINA — Ankle-deep sand blocked the door of their new home. Pushing bicycles through the yard was like wading in a bog. The "lake" part of Miaomiao Lake Village turned out to be nothing but a tiny oasis more than a mile from the cookie-cutter rows of small concrete-block houses.

Ma Shiliang, a village doctor whose family was among some 7,000 Hui Muslims whom the Chinese government had brought to this place from their water-scarce lands in the country's northwest, said officials promised "we would get rich." Instead, these people who once herded sheep and goats over expansive hills now feel like penned-in animals, listless and uncertain of their future.

"If we had known what it was like, we wouldn't have moved here," said Dr. Ma, 41, who, three years on, has been unable to get a job practicing medicine in Miaomiao Lake Village or to find other reliable work.

China calls them "ecological migrants": 329,000 people whom the government had relocated from lands distressed by climate change, industrialization, poor policies and human activity to 161 hastily built villages. They were the fifth wave in an environmental and poverty alleviation program that has resettled 1.14 million residents of the Ningxia Hui Autonomous Region, a territory of dunes and mosques and camels along the ancient Silk Road.

Han Jinlong, the deputy director of migration under Ningxia's Poverty Alleviation and Development Office, said that although the earlier waves were not explicitly labeled ecological migrants, they had also been moved because of the growing harshness of the desert. It is the world's largest environmental migration project.

What China is doing in Ningxia and a few other provinces hit hard by drought and other natural and man-made disasters is a harbinger of actions that governments around the globe, including the United

States, could take as they grapple with climate change, which is expected to displace millions of people in the coming decades.

China has been battered by relentless degradation of the land and worsening weather patterns, including the northern drought. But mass resettlement has brought its own profound problems, embodied in the struggles of the Ma family and their neighbors.

Dr. Ma told me over tea in his living room that each household had to pay a $2,100 "resettlement fee" and was promised a plot of land to farm as the families left behind plentiful fields and animals. But those who received plots ended up having to lease them to an agriculture company, and were left with tiny front yards, where the Mas grow a few chili plants.

The 11-member family was expected to squeeze into a 580-square-foot, two-bedroom home; like many of the migrants, Dr. Ma erected an extra room with white plastic siding in the yard for his parents.

And the officials designing the new homes put toilets in the same

Ten family members, including Dr. Ma's mother, Ma Meihua, center, share the small home.

room as showers, an affront to the Hui Muslims. Dr. Ma dug a pit toilet outside, where the front yard meets the road.

Dr. Ma has not only been unable to get officials to appoint him as a village doctor here, but since November has also failed to find construction work — unstable and low-paying, but the most common job for the village men. The family must live mainly off the $12 per day his wife, Wang Mei, earns in an industrial farm field.

Together with Dr. Ma, three of Dr. Ma's brothers and a nephew brought a total of 38 family members as part of the resettlement. But another brother, Ma Shixiong, was one of a handful who stayed behind in Yejiahe village, a five-hour drive south, defying the government's orders. Officials tore down the homes of the families who left — and punished those who remained by refusing to renovate their houses or build them animal pens, and denying them water pipelines and subsidies for raising sheep and cattle.

Wang Lin, who is also unemployed and was one of eight men I spoke to one afternoon following prayers at Miaomiao Lake's Ji'an Mosque, said he and eight family members planned to return to Yejiahe next year if he did not find a job.

"No one has moved back yet, but people are talking about it," said Mr. Wang, 48. "We can farm the land there. Our homes are no longer there, but we can dig into the earth and build a cave home."

As in much of northern China, most of Ningxia's 26,000 square miles are desert, including the areas chosen for resettlement. Government officials say places like Miaomiao Lake are still an improvement over Xihaigu — the vast region of southern and central Ningxia where the Mas and the other migrants came from — because they are closer to highways; to Yinchuan, Ningxia's capital; and to the Yellow River, a major water source that helped give birth to Chinese civilization.

When Prime Minister Li Keqiang visited Ningxia in February, he told villagers that "relocating impoverished people from bad natural conditions is an important way to alleviate poverty," according to the website of the State Council, China's cabinet.

A third of Ningxia's population — and most of the people who have been resettled — are Hui Muslim. Some Western scholars say that Chinese resettlement policies are at least partly aimed at controlling ethnic minority populations, and that officials may cite environmental reasons as a cover.

Though remote, the parched Xihaigu area has been on the radar of the central government since at least the 1980s, when officials began producing a series of grim reports on the viability of the land. A recent estimate by researchers from the Chinese Academy of Sciences and the Ministry of Land and Resources said the region could sustain only 1.3 million people; the population in 2014 was about 2.3 million.

"The government decided to move people out because the land couldn't feed them," Zhang Jizhong, the deputy director of the Ningxia Poverty Alleviation and Development Office, told me when I met with him and his colleague Mr. Han in their Yinchuan office in August. "The factors are rooted in history, nature and society."

Rainfall was increasingly rare. Villagers had cut down many trees for firewood and to build homes, he said. And the government never built enough reservoirs.

Across Ningxia, the average temperature has risen by 2.1 degrees Celsius, or 3.8 degrees Fahrenheit, in the last 50 years, more than half of that increase occurring from 2001 to 2010, according to a book by Ma Zhongyu, a former senior official, citing data from an international study. Annual precipitation has dropped about 5.7 millimeters, or about a quarter inch, every decade since the 1960s.

Mr. Zhang said a main goal of moving people from Xihaigu was to turn the hills green, with a parallel planting program. More than two million acres have been converted to forest and pasture land, he said, citing the Guyuan area, where forest coverage was 22 percent last year, up from 4 percent in the 1980s.

"There are more wild animals and vegetables there now," Mr. Zhang said of Xihaigu. "When we go there, we can sometimes eat wild chicken."

When the resettlement program was begun in 1983, migrants were given land in the north and told to move and build new homes on their own. These days, the government builds them homes, albeit small ones; of the $3 billion spent on the five waves of relocation, Mr. Zhang said, half was used on the most recent one.

"Houses need to be built well, roads need to be built well, schools need to be built well," he said. "It is all the responsibility of the government."

The relocation process begins with the government asking geological experts to look for sufficient arable land elsewhere in Ningxia, Mr. Zhang said, then gauging whether enough water can be transferred to those places.

The size of each family's yard plot is about 150 square meters, or 1,600 square feet, with the house taking up a third of that. Many complain about the cramped quarters and the additional one mu of farmland — a sixth of an acre — that each person is allotted in most cases, far less than they had in their home villages.

"Land and water are indeed becoming more scarce in the north," Mr. Zhang acknowledged. In the last wave of relocations, a quarter of the families did not get any land, he said, adding that the government had labeled them "labor migrants" and was negotiating with companies to give them city jobs, including as cleaners and security guards.

But officials know that even those who get farmland face a struggle.

"That is far from enough to get you out of poverty," Mr. Zhang said. "It can maybe feed you. The government has been making lots of efforts to get people to be able to work in other sectors, so you don't rely on land itself for a living."

The largest of Ningxia's new migrant villages, Binhe Homeland, has more than 16,000 residents. The smallest have just a few hundred each. Miaomiao Lake is in the middle, with 7,000.

The 1,400 homes there look bland and anonymous, separated by low concrete walls, with only numbers to distinguish them: Dr. Ma's is House 35 in District 5. Most villages have an elementary school, a market area and mosques, but seem more like refugee camps than organic communities.

One afternoon during one of my three recent visits to the region, Ms. Wang, Dr. Ma's wife, came home from the farm to nap during her lunch break. She had been up since dawn spreading fertilizer over a field of watermelons.

After a half-hour's sleep, it was time to return to the desert sun.

She said goodbye to Dr. Ma and their younger children, clad in red-and-white school uniforms. Then she drove an electric cart to a highway, where dozens of other women in electric carts were gathering. Most wore pink head scarves, a shock of color against the sand that stretched to the horizon.

The women clambered onto the flatbeds of two John Deere tractors, which drove off to the watermelon field.

"The work is so exhausting, and I'm dead tired," said Ms. Wang, 39. "I never worked like this before, when we were living in the south. I farmed our own land there, and we lived our days according to our own schedule."

JOSH HANER/THE NEW YORK TIMES

Wang Mei and others leaving for work in the watermelon fields.

I farmed our own land there, and we lived our days according to our own schedule."

Before the move, Ms. Wang imagined that the family would grow food on its own patch of farmland, to eat and sell, as it had done in Yejiahe. But officials decided that the villagers would be better off leasing the plots — a total of 3,300 acres — to a large company, Huatainong Agriculture, and other enterprises because the desert land was hard to farm.

"New immigrants don't really know how to plant crops on the land," explained Wang Zhigang, the director of the Pingluo County poverty alleviation office, adding that migrant families had tried and failed.

Each family member is supposed to receive 195 renminbi per year, or $29, for leasing their land. Mr. Wang said the money is deposited annually in a family bank account, but Dr. Ma said his household had not received the payment after the first year.

So the family's only steady income is the $12 a day Ms. Wang is paid by Huatainong — less than the $15 per day that China says is the average for migrant workers.

Like many in Miaomiao Lake, Dr. Ma has taken out government loans to help meet the family's living expenses.

Dr. Ma learned how to give shots years ago, after watching an older brother whose son got sick frequently. When the village of Yejiahe needed a doctor, that gave him a leg up. His formal education had stopped before high school, but he studied medical techniques on his own. He received his medical license in 2011. He mostly administered vaccines and treated colds and other minor illnesses.

But Dr. Ma said he could not get a job as a doctor in Miaomiao Lake because the government had created only one such post there, which he considered absurd for a village of 7,000. He said that he had repeatedly asked the county health department to add a position for him, but that an official had told him the decision could be made only at a higher level. (A county health official said in an interview that there were plans to add two doctors to Miaomiao Lake.)

Still, friends sometimes ask Dr. Ma to administer a shot. In return, he sometimes asks for the equivalent of $1.50.

One afternoon, a fellow worshiper from Ji'an Mosque came to Dr. Ma's home for an intravenous drip of calcium gluconate, a mineral supplement. The man lay on a bed by the front window and held out his right arm. The doctor worked with precision — and without charge.

It is difficult to get a handle on employment in Miaomiao Lake. Mr. Wang, the Pingluo County official, said of the 2,000 ecological migrants in the village who had "the ability to work," 93 percent had jobs. A senior executive at Huatainong said the company employed 400 to 500 women for half the year, and about 100 at other times. Dr. Ma and many others disputed the official employment figures, saying that most men could not find regular work on construction projects in the new villages or nearby cities.

Once each year, residents said, government officials have offered training sessions of one to two hours to teach villagers how to become welders or bricklayers. "Useless," Dr. Ma said. "There aren't many jobs available."

City-level officials visited the village for a day in May; Dr. Ma said one offered him a job in a coal-washing factory in a city, but he "didn't want to go because the lifestyle there is different than ours," with few Hui Muslims and many ethnic Han.

There was also the matter of pride. "I've been a village doctor," he said. "You can't just make me a coal-mine worker now. It's not appropriate."

Unable or unwilling to do manual or farm work, some of the migrants run restaurants, pharmacies or other small businesses. Near the front archway of the village is a plaza lined with storefronts, but most were shuttered the morning I visited. No one was renting them.

I found Ma Nüwa in the only open shop along one row. She had been selling blankets there for more than two years, and said she made about $75 per month.

"Business is bad; there are no people here," she said. "I have three boys. My husband has to go outside to find manual labor."

Some out-of-work men retreat to the mosques, where five daily prayers give life some structure. Sometimes before going to pray, Dr. Ma showers, puts on a crisp white shirt and fixes his skullcap just right, adjusting it in the mirror.

At his home, there are always children around. The parents took the youngest daughter, Shuyun, out of preschool because they could not afford the $150 fee each semester. The oldest, 16-year-old Xiaofang, had been enrolled in a boarding school, but stopped after a year and a half.

"I don't like school, and I don't want to go back," she told me one day as she cooked noodles for the family for lunch. "I plan to go to Yinchuan after Ramadan to find work."

But Dr. Ma said: "My oldest daughter isn't going to Yinchuan. She's too young." The road to the Mas' old village, Yejiahe, winds uphill past a reservoir, past hills covered with soft yellow silt, past horses and haystacks in people's yards. The landscape is wide and rolling and green, nothing like Miaomiao Lake.

We parked atop a ridge overlooking a valley. Dr. Ma's brother Ma Shixiong greeted me at the side of the road, dressed in a blue tunic and skullcap. His face had as many creases as the hills.

He was the man who stayed behind, even as his extended clan, including his elderly parents, had migrated northward. His wife, three of his sons and four grandchildren also remained in Yejiahe; two other sons worked at a restaurant in Beijing. About 300 villagers remained from a population of about 1,400 in the late 1990s.

He handed me a cup of tea in a front room with a brick floor and mud walls that, even in the summer heat, stayed cool.

"We didn't have any plans to move out there," Mr. Ma, 50, said of Miaomiao Lake. "We knew we would only be given one house."

He told me many Yejiahe families had a long history of being relocated at the whims of government officials. His ancestors lived in south-central Ningxia, near the Yellow River, "a very easy place to live," he said. More than 100 years ago, officials under the Qing court ordered the family to move to Yejiahe.

Decades ago, Communist officials divided the village into five teams. The Mas were in one called Xiahe. A few years ago, officials told the Xiahe families they had to relocate to the north. Fifty households moved; nine refused.

Why some chose to stay, even at the cost of fracturing extended families, became clear once Mr. Ma walked me through his home.

Compared with his brother's place in Miaomiao Lake, it might as well have been an imperial palace. Two rows of rooms face a large courtyard. The families of two of his sons, each with two children, have their own quarters. The total area is 300 square meters — 3,229 square feet, twice the size of the housing plots in the new village.

Mr. Ma said he had visited his family a half-dozen times in Miaomiao Lake, before their ailing father died in February 2015.

"When I first saw that place — that little yard and the little house and the little bathroom in front of the door..." he said, trailing off. "The hygiene is not good. It's not a very civil lifestyle."

"You don't have land, and you need to go out to find jobs," he added. "How can you make a living?"

In Yejiahe, Mr. Ma had up to eight acres of land to farm, though occasional floods had destroyed some fields. Behind his home was a large field of corn and oats. The family sold those crops as well as potatoes and millet. In front of the house, a donkey stood in a pen.

The family drew water from a well in the back, as villagers had done for generations. The people who moved to Miaomiao Lake had been relieved to finally get running water. Then they heard that soon after they moved, pipelines for tap water had been installed for much of their former village.

But not for the Xiahe team members who defied the government relocation order. It was as if they were phantom households, Mr. Ma said, wiped from existence. As we talked, neighbors began crowding into the front room. They had heard that a reporter from Beijing was in town. Each wanted to voice a complaint about local corruption. "It's a primitive society here because no one cares about us," Mr. Ma said.

The day was fading, and Mr. Ma led me outside to see his brothers' old homes. We climbed up a hill, and the wide valley stretched out in front of us. Mr. Ma and his neighbors said the area had been drying up for years; there was less rain than a decade ago.

But I could see patches of vegetation on the hills. Since the Xiahe team left, trees and shrubs had begun to reappear, Mr. Ma said. Fewer people meant less stress on the land.

We reached a rise above the valley. In front of me was what remained of the mud-wall home where Dr. Ma and Ms. Wang had begun raising seven children. Officials had it knocked down, leaving blocks of earth and crumbling walls in the dirt.

For Ma Shixiong, the memory of his four brothers' departure in November 2013 was as clear as the sky overhead. The families had loaded their furniture onto trucks. They had boarded a bus the next morning.

"We all cried," Mr. Ma said. "They cried, I cried. We were a family, and now we're separated. I hope they will move back, but it's impossible."

We walked back down the ridge. The afternoon shadows were lengthening, and the homes on the hill stood silent in their ruin.

KIKI ZHAO AND SARAH LI CONTRIBUTED RESEARCH.

PRODUCED BY CRAIG ALLEN, GRAY BELTRAN, HANNAH FAIRFIELD, DAVID FURST, TAIGE JENSEN, MEAGHAN LOORAM, AND JEREMY WHITE.

# Heat, Hunger and War Force Africans Onto a 'Road of Fire'

BY SOMINI SENGUPTA  |  DEC. 15, 2016

AGADEZ, NIGER — The world dismisses them as economic migrants. The law treats them as criminals who show up at a nation's borders uninvited. Prayers alone protect them on the journey across the merciless Sahara.

But peel back the layers of their stories and you find a complex bundle of trouble and want that prompts the men and boys of West Africa to leave home, endure beatings and bribes, board a smuggler's pickup truck and try to make a living far, far away.

They do it because the rains have become so fickle, the days measurably hotter, the droughts more frequent and more fierce, making it impossible to grow enough food on their land. Some go to the cities first, only to find jobs are scarce. Some come from countries ruled by dictators, like Gambia, whose longtime ruler recently refused to accept the results of an election he lost. Others come from countries crawling with jihadists, like Mali.

In Agadez, a fabled gateway town of sand and hustle through which hundreds of thousands exit the Sahel on their way abroad, I met dozens of them. One was Bori Bokoum, 21, from a village in the Mopti region of Mali. Fighters for Al Qaeda clash with government forces in the area, one of many reasons making a living had become much harder than in his father's time.

One bad harvest followed another, he said. Not enough rice and millet could be eked out of the soil. So, as a teenager, he ventured out to sell watches in the nearest market town for a while, then worked on a farm in neighboring Ivory Coast, saving up for this journey. Libya was his destination, then maybe across the Mediterranean Sea, to Italy.

"To try my luck," was how Mr. Bokoum put it. "I know it's difficult. But everyone goes. I also have to try."

This journey has become a rite of passage for West Africans of his generation. The slow burn of climate change makes subsistence farming, already risky business in a hot, arid region, even more of a gamble. Pressures on land and water fuel clashes, big and small. Insurgencies simmer across the region, prompting United States counterterrorism forces to keep watch from a base on the outskirts of Agadez.

This year, more than 311,000 people have passed through Agadez on their way to either Algeria or Libya, and some onward to Europe, according to the International Organization for Migration. The largest numbers are from Niger and its West African neighbors, including Mr. Bokoum's home, Mali.

Scholars of migration count people like Mr. Bokoum among the millions who could be displaced around the world in coming decades as rising seas, widening deserts and erratic weather threaten traditional livelihoods. For the men who pour through Agadez, these hardships are tangled up with intense economic, political and demographic pressures.

"Climate change on its own doesn't force people to move but it amplifies pre-existing vulnerabilities," said Jane McAdam, an Australian law professor who studies the trend. They move when they can no longer imagine a future living off their land — or as she said, "when life becomes increasingly intolerable."

But many of these people fall through the cracks of international law. The United Nations 1951 refugee convention applies only to those fleeing war and persecution, and even that treaty's obligation to offer protection is increasingly flouted by many countries wary of foreigners.

In such a political climate, policy makers point out, the chances of expanding the law to include those displaced by environmental degradation are slim to none. It explains why the more than 100 countries that have ratified the Paris climate agreement this year acknowledged that environmental changes would spur the movement of people, but kicked the can down the road on what to do about them.

## A BARREN OUTLOOK

Many migrants pass through Agadez from the villages around Zinder, a city roughly situated between the mouth of the Sahara and Niger's border with Nigeria. Until 1926, Zinder was Niger's capital. Then it ran low on water.

Early one gray-yellow morning, I set off from Zinder for a village called Chana, the home of one of the migrants I had met, Habibou Idi. Rows upon rows of millet grew on both sides of the two-lane national highway, punctuated occasionally by a spindly acacia. About an hour outside the city, some boys were raking the soil, yanking out weeds.

An older man sitting to the side said that back when he was a boy, the millet stood so high that you could hardly see workers in the fields. Midway through the growing season, it now barely reaches their knees.

An hour farther out of the city, we veered off the paved road and across a barren, rutted field.

In Chana, there was a steady thud of women pounding beans with wooden pestles. The beans grew along the ground, in the shade of the millet. They were the only crop ready for harvest. And so the people of Chana ate beans, morning and night: beans pounded, boiled, flavored with salt.

As Mr. Idi, 33, led me through his fields, he recalled hearing stories of what Chana looked like before a great drought swept across the Sahel in the 1970s and 1980s. The village was encircled by trees, he was told.

Back then, like most villagers, his father had a cow and plenty of sheep. Their droppings fertilized the land. Today, Mr. Idi said, not a single cow is left in Chana. They were sold to buy food.

Mr. Idi complained that the rains are now hard to predict. Sometimes they come in May, and he rushes out to plant his millet and beans, only to find the clouds closing up and his crops withering. Even when a good rain comes, it just floods. Most of the trees are gone, they were cut for firewood.

Living off the land is no longer an option, so unlike his father or grandfather before him, Mr. Idi has spent the last several years working across the border in Nigeria — hauling goods, watering gardens, whatever he could find.

This summer, for the first time, he boarded a bus to Agadez, and then a truck across the dunes to Algeria. There, he mostly begged.

He lasted only a few months.

The Algerian authorities rounded up hundreds of Nigeriens and deposited them back in Agadez.

That is where I met him, in a line for the bus back to Chana. Sand filled the breast pocket of his tunic. He was bringing home a blanket, a collection of secondhand clothes and 50,000 CFAs (the local currency, pronounced SAY-fas), worth about $100.

That did not last long, either. Mr. Idi arrived home to find that his family had taken out a loan of nearly the same amount in his absence. They had sold four of their five goats, too. There were many mouths to feed: his wife, their four children, plus his late brother's seven.

## HOTTER HOTS AND UNPREDICTABLE RAINS

Sub-Saharan Africa is in the throes of a population boom, which means that people have to grow more food precisely at a time when climate change is making it all the more difficult. Fertility rates remain higher than in other parts of the world, and Niger has the highest in the entire world: Women bear more than seven children on average.

Once every three years, according to scientists from the Famine Early Warning Systems Network, or FEWS Net, Niger faces food insecurity, or a lack of adequate food to eat. Hunger here is among the worst in the world: About 45 percent of Niger's children under 5 suffer from chronic malnutrition.

Meanwhile, in what is already one of the hottest places on Earth, it has gotten steadily hotter: by 0.7 degrees Celsius since 1975, Fews Net has found. Other places in the world are warming faster, for sure. But this is the Sahel, where daytime highs often soar well above 45 degrees Celsius (113 Fahrenheit) and growing food in sandy, inhospitable soil is already difficult.

Niger's neighbors share many of those woes. In Mali, temperatures have gone up by 0.8 degrees Celsius since 1975. Summer rains have increased, but are not at the levels they were before the drought.

In Chad, temperatures have risen by 0.8 degrees Celsius in the same period, according to FEWS Net. The group, which is financed with United States assistance, has warned that cereal production could drop by 30 percent per capita by 2025.

Chad is where FEWS Net's chief representative for the Sahel, a meteorologist named Alkhalil Adoum, was born in 1957. As a boy, he loved running through the blinding rains of summer, when you couldn't even see what was ahead of you. He knew a good rain would fill the savanna with wild fruit, and the first green shoots of sorghum would taste as sweet as sugar cane. His family's cows, once they ate new grass, would give more milk.

"You love the first rains," Mr. Adoum said. "You know, as a kid, there's better times ahead."

Those rains don't come anymore, he said.

There are conflicting scientific models about the effects of climate change on precipitation: some say much of sub-Saharan Africa will be wetter; others drier. The main points of agreement is that the rainy season will be more unpredictable and more intense. On top of that, the hottest parts of the continent will get hotter.

Extreme heat can have grievous consequences on food and disease, the World Food Program found in a survey of scientific studies. Malaria-carrying mosquitoes thrive in it. Pests are more likely to attack crops. Corn and wheat yields decline.

A study, published in December by the International Monitoring Displacement Center, found that in 2015 alone, sudden-onset disaster displaced 1.1 million people in Africa from one part of their country to another.

And then there is the competition over water. Already, it sets off clashes between farmers and herders, often hardened by ethnic divisions. A growing body of research suggests that local droughts, especially in poor, vulnerable countries, heighten the risk of civil conflict.

Risk analysts, including at the London-based firm Verisk Maplecroft, conclude that climate change amplifies the risks of civil unrest across the entire midsection of sub-Saharan Africa, from Mali in the west to Ethiopia in the East.

A grisly example lies in full display just a few hours by road from Mr. Idi's village. In the southeastern corner of the country, where Niger meets Nigeria, Chad and Cameroon, more than 270,000 people huddle for safety from the Boko Haram insurgency. Altogether, across the Lake Chad Basin, 2.4 million people have fled their homes, according to the United Nations.

## A CITY OF DREAMS

Agadez is a city of mud-brick compounds with high walls and blazing bright metal doors. For centuries, it was filled with traders and nomads. In recent decades, it was a tourist magnet, until ethnic rebellions and then jihadist violence drove people away.

Today, migration is the main industry. Drivers, smugglers, money changers, sex workers, police officers — everyone lives off the men on the move. It is a city of dreams, both budding and broken. It is where the journey across the desert begins for so many young West African men, and it is where the journey ends, when they fail.

The smugglers' den where I found Mr. Bokoum, the 21-year-old from Mali, was a set of two adjoining courtyards, with two concrete-floored rooms. Upside-down jerrycans served as stools, plastic mats as sofas.

He had been in Agadez for three months, waiting for his mother to send him money. It can cost 350,000 CFAs — about $600 — to get from Agadez to the Libyan border, on the back of a pickup truck.

The smugglers had also started out as migrants, and most of them worked for a while in Libya. Now, they make money off other men's journeys. None would hint at how much.

Mohamed Diallo, a Senegalese manager of the compound, blamed Western countries for spewing carbon into the atmosphere, and he was skeptical of their leaders' promises to curb emissions.

"The big powers are polluting and creating problems for us," he said. He was appalled that Africans trying to go to Europe were treated like criminals, when Europeans in Africa were treated like kings.

Mr. Diallo's compound, like others in Agadez, has a weekly rhythm.

He instructs those seeking to make the journey to Libya to be inside by Sunday night. Monday morning, he treats them to a feast before the long haul. He roasts a sheep, plays some music, turns on the ceiling fans for a couple of hours.

Just after sundown, a white Toyota pickup pulls up. Monday night is when Nigerien soldiers change shifts, heading out of Agadez and into a desert outpost. The Toyotas follow, stopping briefly at the police checkpoint at the edge of the city before speeding into the dunes. Those who fall off the trucks are left behind.

The journey to the Libyan border, 250 miles in all, takes three days. No one knows how many die along the way.

Those who venture a journey across the Mediterranean take a deadly gamble, too. Among the more than 4,700 people who have died trying to cross the Central Mediterranean so far in 2016, the vast majority cannot be identified. Of those who can, Africans make up the largest share.

"The migrant road," Mr. Diallo said, "is a road on fire."

### 'I WILL BE A BURDEN TO THEM'

Those who make it to Libya do not necessarily make it inside Libya. It is a lawless country where some migrants get thrown behind bars — and some, according to human rights groups, are raped and tortured by militias demanding money. Some run out of money, or heart, to continue the journey to Europe.

On the way back, they usually knock on the gates of the International Organization for Migration's transit center at the edge of Agadez.

There were about 400 boys and men there the week I visited. They lounged on thin rose-print mattresses. They played cards and scrolled through their phones, calling home if they had any credit left. A few attended a class on how to start a business; others rested in the medical ward.

The mix of shame and boredom hung so heavy you could practically smell it. One young man walked around with an open wound on his elbow; he vaguely said he was injured in a brawl in Libya.

When the heat of the day broke, they roused themselves and played soccer.

The migrants from the countryside all had similar stories. Their fathers had never left the land — they all felt they had to. The harvest was not enough; their families had no tractors, just lazy donkeys. Work in nearby towns brought in a fraction of what they figured they could make abroad.

The lure of abroad, Algeria or Libya or beyond, was strong. Facebook posts from friends and neighbors made it seem like a cakewalk.

Ibrahim Diarra said that fickle rains made it too hard to grow peanuts and corn on the family farm in the Tambacounda region of Senegal. He watched the young men of his village leave, each pulled by the stories of those who went before. Then he followed.

Mr. Diarra made his way through Qaeda-riddled northern Mali, then worked construction for six months in Mauritania, before pushing on to Tamanrasset, in Algeria. If he could just get to Morocco, he had heard, he could climb over a fence and be in Spain.

"They told me it's very easy," he said.

It wasn't. He lasted two months in Algeria. Then, he went back to Agadez and asked the migration organization for a bus ticket home. So far this year, 100,000 people have made the same reverse journey.

On a Thursday — departure night for those whose emigration dreams are dashed — bittersweet chaos erupted in the courtyard as two large buses pulled up.

The manager of the transit center, Azaoua Mahamen, sat on the porch with his laptop open, scrolling through the names of those who had been cleared to go home. Migrants need identity papers, and government permission. If they are children, Mr. Mahamen has to make sure they have a family to go back to; a few don't.

Dozens of young men crowded around him, their eyes like headlights in the dark. They shouted their names. They waved their identity cards, wrapped in plastic. One group complained that only Guineans were getting out that night. The Ivory Coast contingent started cheering when one of their compatriots was called.

Mr. Diarra listened for his name, though he wasn't looking forward to facing his parents empty-handed.

"I'm supposed to support my family," he explained. "Now I have no clothes, nothing. I will be a burden to them."

His father, especially, would be upset. "He'll ask me how my friends got to Europe and I came back," he said, shaking his head.

He said he would try the journey again. It would take him a few months to cobble together the money.

PRODUCED BY CRAIG ALLEN, GRAY BELTRAN, JOE BURGESS, HANNAH FAIRFIELD, DAVID FURST, TAIGE JENSEN AND MEAGHAN LOORAM

# As Donald Trump Denies Climate Change, These Kids Die of It

OPINION | BY NICHOLAS KRISTOF | JAN. 6, 2017

TSIHOMBE, MADAGASCAR — She is just a frightened mom, worrying if her son will survive, and certainly not fretting about American politics — for she has never heard of either President Obama or Donald Trump.

What about America itself? Ranomasy, who lives in an isolated village on this island of Madagascar off southern Africa, shakes her head. It doesn't ring any bells.

Yet we Americans may be inadvertently killing her infant son. Climate change, disproportionately caused by carbon emissions from America, seems to be behind a severe drought that has led crops to wilt across seven countries in southern Africa. The result is acute malnutrition for 1.3 million children in the region, the United Nations says.

Trump has repeatedly mocked climate change, once even calling it a hoax fabricated by China. But climate change here is as tangible as its victims. Trump should come and feel these children's ribs and watch them struggle for life. It's true that the links between our carbon emissions and any particular drought are convoluted, but over all, climate change is as palpable as a wizened, glassy-eyed child dying of starvation. Like Ranomasy's 18-month-old son, Tsapasoa.

Southern Africa's drought and food crisis have gone largely unnoticed around the world. The situation has been particularly severe in Madagascar, a lovely island nation known for deserted sandy beaches and playful long-tailed primates called lemurs.

But the southern part of the island doesn't look anything like the animated movie "Madagascar": Families are slowly starving because rains and crops have failed for the last few years. They are reduced to eating cactus and even rocks or ashes. The United Nations estimates that nearly one million people in Madagascar alone need emergency food assistance.

I met Ranomasy at an emergency feeding station run by Catholic nuns who were trying to save her baby. Ranomasy had carried Tsapasoa 12 hours on a trek through the desert to get to the nuns, walking barefoot because most villagers have already sold everything from shoes to spoons to survive.

"I feel so powerless as a mother, because I know how much I love my child," she said. "But whatever I do just doesn't work."

The drought is also severe in Lesotho, Malawi, Mozambique, Swaziland, Zambia and Zimbabwe, and a related drought has devastated East Africa and the Horn of Africa and is expected to continue this year. The U.N. World Food Program has urgently appealed for assistance, but only half the money needed has been donated.

The immediate cause of the droughts was an extremely warm El Niño event, which came on top of a larger drying trend in the last few decades in parts of Africa. New research, just published in the bulletin of the American Meteorological Society, concludes that human-caused

NICHOLAS KRISTOF/THE NEW YORK TIMES

Ranomasy walked 12 hours to get her 18-month-old son, Tsapasoa, to an emergency feeding station.

climate change exacerbated El Niño's intensity and significantly reduced rainfall in parts of Ethiopia and southern Africa.

The researchers calculated that human contributions to global warming reduced water runoff in southern Africa by 48 percent and concluded that these human contributions "have contributed to substantial food crises."

As an American, I'm proud to see U.S. assistance saving lives here. If it weren't for U.S.A.I.D., the American aid agency, and non-profit groups like Catholic Relief Services that work in these villages, far more cadavers would be piling up. But my pride is mixed with guilt: The United States single-handedly accounts for more than one-quarter of the world's carbon dioxide emissions over the last 150 years, more than twice as much as any other country.

The basic injustice is that we rich countries produced the carbon that is devastating impoverished people from Madagascar to Bangladesh. In America, climate change costs families beach homes;

Many rivers and wells have dried up in southern Madagascar.

in poor countries, parents lose their children.

In one Madagascar hamlet I visited, villagers used to get water from a well a three-hour walk away, but then it went dry. Now they hike the three hours and then buy water from a man who trucks it in. But they have almost no money. Not one of the children in the village has ever had a bath.

Families in this region traditionally raised cattle, but many have sold their herds to buy food to survive. Selling pressure has sent the price of a cow tumbling from $300 to less than $100.

Families are also pulling their children out of school, to send them foraging for edible plants. In one village I visited, fewer than 15 percent of the children are attending primary school this year.

One of the children who dropped out is Fombasoa, who should be in the third grade but now spends her days scouring the desert for a wild red cactus fruit. Fombasoa's family is also ready to marry her off, even

NICHOLAS KRISTOF/THE NEW YORK TIMES

Fombasoa, 10, at left. Her father would like to marry her off, because then her husband would be responsible for feeding her.

though she is just 10, because then her husband would be responsible for feeding her.

"If I can find her a husband, I would marry her," said her father, Sonjona, who, like many villagers, has just one name. "But these days there is no man who wants her" — because no one can afford the bride price of about $32.

Sonjona realizes that it is wrong to marry off a 10-year-old, but he also knows it is wrong to see his daughter starve. "I feel despair," he said. "I don't feel a man any more. I used to have muscles; now I have only bones. I feel guilty, because my job was to care for my children, and now they have only red cactus fruit."

Other families showed me how they pick rocks of chalk from the ground, break them into dust and cook the dust into soup. "It fills our stomachs at least," explained Limbiaza, a 20-year-old woman in one remote village. As it becomes more difficult to find the chalk rocks, some families make soup from ashes from old cooking fires.

Scientists used to think that the horror of starvation was principally the dying children. Now they understand there is a far broader toll: When children in utero and in the first few years of life are malnourished, their brains don't develop properly. As a result, they may suffer permanently impaired brain function.

"If children are stunted and do not receive the nutrition and attention in these first 1,000 days, it is very difficult to catch back up," noted Joshua Poole, the Madagascar director of Catholic Relief Services. "Nutritional neglect during this critical period prevents children from reaching their full mental potential."

For the next half century or so, we will see students learning less in school and economies held back, because in 2017 we allowed more than a million kids to be malnourished just here in southern Africa, collateral damage from our carbon-intensive way of life.

The struggling people of Madagascar are caught between their own corrupt, ineffective government, which denies the scale of the crisis, and overseas governments that don't want to curb carbon emissions.

Whatever we do to limit the growth of carbon, climate problems will worsen for decades to come. Those of us in the rich world who have emitted most of the carbon bear a special responsibility to help people like these Madagascar villagers who are simultaneously least responsible for climate change and most vulnerable to it.

The challenges are not hopeless, and I saw programs here that worked. The World Food Program runs school feeding programs that use local volunteers and, at a cost of 25 cents per child per day, give children a free daily meal that staves off starvation and creates an incentive to keep children in school.

We need these emergency relief efforts — and constant vigilance to intervene early to avert famines — but we can also do far more to help local people help themselves.

Catholic Relief Services provides emergency food aid, but it also promotes drought-resistant seed varieties and is showing farmers near the coast how to fish. It is also working with American scientists on new technologies to supply water in Madagascar, using condensation or small-scale desalination.

American technology helped create the problem, and it would be nice to see American technology used more aggressively to mitigate the burden on the victims.

For me, the most wrenching sight of this trip was of two starving boys near the southern tip of Madagascar. Their parents are climate refugees who fled their village to try to find a way to survive, leaving the boys in the care of an aunt, even though she doesn't have enough food for her own two daughters.

I met the boys, Fokondraza, 5, and Voriavy, 3, in the evening, and they said that so far that day they hadn't eaten or drunk anything (the closest well, producing somewhat salty water, is several hours away by foot, and fetching a pail of water becomes more burdensome when everyone is malnourished and anemic). Their aunt, Fideline, began to prepare the day's meal.

She broke off cactus pads, scraped off the thorns and boiled them briefly, and the boys ate them — even though they provide little nutrition. "My heart is breaking because I have nothing to give them," Fideline said. "I have no choice."

At night, the boys sometimes cry from hunger, she said. But that is a good sign. When a person is near starvation, the body shuts down emotion, becoming zombielike as every calorie goes to keeping the heart and lungs working. It is the children who don't cry, those quiet and expressionless, who are at greatest risk — and the two boys are becoming more like that.

I don't pretend that the links between climate change and this food crisis are simple, or that the solutions are straightforward. I flew halfway around the world and then drove for two days to get to these villages, pumping out carbon the whole way.

Yet we do know what will help in the long run: sticking with the Paris agreement to limit global warming, as well as with President Obama's Clean Power Plan. We must also put a price on carbon and invest much more heavily in research on renewable energy.

In the short and medium term, we must step up assistance to climate refugees and sufferers, both to provide relief and to assist with new livelihoods that adjust to new climate realities. (For individuals who want to help, the organization most active in the areas I visited was Catholic Relief Services, which accepts donations for southern Madagascar.)

The most basic starting point is for the American president-elect to acknowledge what even illiterate Madagascar villagers understand: Climate change is real.

As the sun set, I told Fideline that there was a powerful man named Trump half a world away, in a country she had never heard of, who just might be able to have some impact, over many years, on the climate here. I asked her what she would tell him.

"I would ask him to do what he can, so that once more I can grow cassava, corn, black-eyed peas and sorghum," she said. "We're desperate."

Mr. President-elect, are you listening?

# How a Warming Planet Drives Human Migration

BY JESSICA BENKO  |  APRIL 19, 2017

CLIMATE CHANGE is not equally felt across the globe, and neither are its longer term consequences. This map overlays human turmoil — represented here by United Nations data on nearly 64 million "persons of concern," whose numbers have tripled since 2005 — with climate turmoil, represented by data from NASA's Common Sense Climate Index. The correlation is striking.

Climate change is a threat multiplier: It contributes to economic and political instability and also worsens the effects. It propels sudden-onset disasters like floods and storms and slow-onset disasters like drought and desertification; those disasters contribute to failed crops, famine and overcrowded urban centers; those crises inflame political unrest and worsen the impacts of war, which leads to even more displacement. There is no internationally recognized legal definition for "environmental migrants" or "climate refugees," so there is no formal reckoning of how many have left their homes because climate change has made their lives or livelihoods untenable. In a 2010 Gallup World Poll, though, about 12 percent of respondents — representing a total of 500 million adults — said severe environmental problems would require them to move within the next five years.

## 1. AMAZON BASIN

As glacial melting reduces freshwater reserves for the Andean plain, tensions are growing between locals and the mining and agribusiness operations that consume much of what remains. Researchers predict that this resource conflict will drive more migrants to the Amazon Basin where many have already turned to informal mining and coca cultivation, fueling the rise of criminal syndicates.

## 2. LAKE CHAD

A vital resource for Cameroon, Chad, Niger and Nigeria, Lake Chad has shrunk by more than 90 percent since 1963. The ecological catastrophe is a compounding factor in the Boko Haram insurgency crisis, which has led to the displacement of 3.5 million people.

## 3. SYRIA

In 2007, eastern Syria — along with Turkey, northern Iraq and western Iran — entered a three-year drought, the region's worst since scientists began measuring them. In Syria, water scarcity, crop failures and livestock deaths drove an estimated 1.5 million people to the cities from rural areas. Food prices soared, contributing to economic and social tensions and leaving Syrians dangerously vulnerable to the subsequent war.

## 4. CHINA

The country's deserts have expanded by 21,000 square miles since 1975, crowding out cropland and producing devastating sandstorms. The government has resettled hundreds of thousands of "ecological migrants" — many of them religious or ethnic minorities — from across the affected areas of northern China.

## 5. PHILIPPINES

Many climate models predict that warming oceans will make typhoons and tropical storms more intense, raising their destructive potential. Since 2013, nearly 15 million people have been displaced by typhoons and storms in the Philippines. The deadliest of them, Typhoon Haiyan, killed more than 7,000 people.

# Climate Change Is Driving People From Home. So Why Don't They Count as Refugees?

BY SOMINI SENGUPTA | DEC. 21, 2017

UNITED NATIONS — More than 65 million people are displaced from their homes, the largest number since the Second World War, and nearly 25 million of them are refugees and asylum seekers living outside their own country.

But that number doesn't include people displaced by climate change.

Under international law, only those who have fled their countries because of war or persecution are entitled to refugee status. People forced to leave home because of climate change, or who leave because climate change has made it harder for them to make a living, don't qualify.

The law doesn't offer them much protection at all unless they can show they are fleeing a war zone or face a fear of persecution if they are returned home.

## IS A LEGAL DEFINITION OUTDATED?

That's not surprising, perhaps: The treaty that defines the status of refugees was written at the end of World War II.

A research paper, published Thursday in Science magazine, suggests that weather shocks are spurring people to seek asylum in the European Union. The researchers found that over a 15-year period, asylum applications in Europe increased along with "hotter-than-normal temperatures" in the countries where the asylum seekers had come from.

They predict that many more people will seek asylum in Europe as temperatures in their home countries are projected to rise.

The paper, by Anouch Missirian and Wolfram Schlenker, looks at weather patterns in the countries of origin for asylum applicants between 2000 and 2014. It found that "weather shocks in agricultural regions in 103 countries around the globe directly influence emigration" to Europe.

"Part of the flow," said Dr. Schlenker, a professor at the School of International and Public Affairs at Columbia University and a co-author of the study, "we can explain by what happens to the weather in the source country."

## WHY ISN'T ANYONE PROPOSING A NEW LAW?

For starters, refugee advocates fear that if the 1951 refugee treaty were opened for renegotiation, politicians in various countries would try to weaken the protections that exist now. That includes the Trump administration, which has barred people from eight countries — including refugees from war-torn Syria and Yemen — from coming into the country altogether.

A group of academics and advocates has spent the last two years proposing an entirely new treaty, with new categories to cover those who are forcibly displaced, including by the ravages of climate change. Michael W. Doyle, a Columbia professor leading the effort to draft a new treaty, said he didn't expect a new treaty to be embraced anytime soon, but insisted that those conversations should start as record numbers of people leave their home countries and end up displaced in others, often without legal status.

"In the modern world," Dr. Doyle said, "people are fleeing for their lives for a variety of reasons."

## TRIAL BALLOONS HAVE BEEN FLOATED

A New Zealand lawmaker recently proposed a special visa category for people displaced by climate change. "One of the options is a special humanitarian visa to allow people who are forced to migrate because of climate change," the minister, James Shaw, said in an interview from a global climate summit in Bonn, Germany, in November.

Mr. Shaw has said nothing since then about when legislation might be proposed, and it's far from clear whether it would pass.

Several countries have offered humanitarian visas in the aftermath of calamitous natural disasters, including the United States after hurricanes and earthquakes, including in Haiti in 2010. (The Trump administration ended that so-called protected status for Haitians in November.)

## THERE'S A BIGGER PROBLEM

As Elizabeth Ferris, a professor at Georgetown University, points out, most people whose lands and livelihoods are ravaged by either natural disaster or the slow burn of climate change aren't likely to leave their countries. Many more will move somewhere else within their own country — from the countryside to cities, for instance, or from low-lying areas prone to flooding to higher elevation.

Indeed, natural disasters forced an estimated 24 million people to be displaced within the borders of their own country in 2016, according to the latest report by the Internal Displacement Monitoring Center.

# Running Dry in Cape Town

**OPINION | BY DIANNA KANE | FEB. 1, 2018**

CAPE TOWN — This city celebrated for its natural beauty on South Africa's southwest coast is about to run out of water.

Starting Thursday, we're being asked to curb our use of municipal water to 13.2 gallons a day. If water levels keep falling as expected, this will be reduced to 6.6 gallons on April 16, referred to here as Day Zero, when most taps are expected to be shut off and residents will have to line up at 200 distribution points for their daily allotment. In the lead-up to Day Zero, those who don't abide by the restrictions will face fines and may have water-monitoring devices placed on their properties.

Yes, this is actually happening in South Africa's second-most populous city, a sprawling metropolis with nearly four million people.

Already, we have buckets under every faucet to capture water from hand washing, teeth brushing and food washing. This becomes the gray water we use to flush our toilets once or twice a day. Cafes and restaurants have signs asking customers to flush only when necessary. Showering has become a special (and rare) ritual; radio stations have put out playlists of songs lasting two minutes to help bathers keep it quick. Clothes are worn multiple times before washing; people try

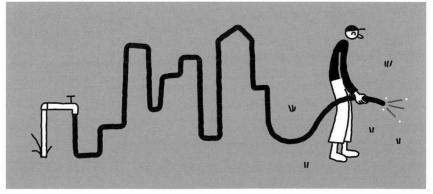

DANIEL SAVAGE

to keep their sheets clean longer by washing their feet before getting into bed. Some restaurants and gyms have replaced sinks with hand-sanitizing stations.

The Western Cape Province, where Cape Town is, has been in severe drought for three years. The water shortage has been amplified by the population boom here; more than a million new residents have arrived in the city in the past 15 years. The city's desperate attempts to build desalination plants and install new groundwater pumps may help, but these solutions seem to be the equivalent of building an extra lane on an already jammed highway. The underlying causes of the shortage are likely to continue to stress the system. Other cities in drought-prone regions should pay close attention.

I've been living in Cape Town on and off for the past 15 years. The rest of the time, I live in San Francisco. California experienced its own multiyear drought, which ended in early 2017, so I've watched both places struggle with the issues of population growth, resource management and climate change.

For all the hardships here, I find many of the elements of this new lifestyle deeply satisfying. They have challenged our middle-class consumption patterns and expectations that "modern life" should yield certain blind comforts and conveniences. When you start thinking about water in small, specific quantities, seeing how much gray water it takes to flush offers a clear sense of how much drinking water we've been flushing away. The average bathtub here holds about 20 gallons — equivalent to about three days' worth of water for one person under Day Zero rules.

There are many people who still aren't doing enough to curb usage, but in a city of high inequality and concentrated wealth and privilege, there's a leveling that's happening. Behaviors have changed quickly and on a broad scale. The city has published maps that indicate which households are above or below the recommended water consumption level. It's now commonplace to see an unflushed toilet in a fancy restaurant, per guidelines that advise, "When it's yellow, let it

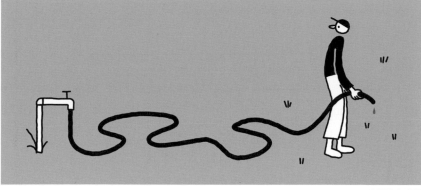

mellow." I find this motivating; it's evidence of a collective consciousness and effort.

In addition to the idea that population growth has collided with drought and climate change, there's a feeling that water has been too cheap for too long and that the city hasn't done enough to upgrade its infrastructure. Leaking water pipes are a major problem. Apparently this is true for many cities, but it is unacceptable in a world where resources are increasingly scarce and stretched thin.

There's also a sense here that this crisis isn't going to be a one-time event with a quick fix. Even with upgrades to the water system, the larger question is: How do we rethink our relationship to water and plan for next 50, 100 and 200 years? On a global scale, we need to reimagine how we live and use our resources. We should be asking ourselves how might we redesign our homes and cities to make conservation efforts easier and optimize our natural resources for the long term on a large scale.

As we have learned here in this crisis, homes should be built with rain water tanks to supply washing machines and water pipes to pump used water from those machines into toilets. We also need clearer feedback on our own habits. Water meters should be brought inside the house so we see how our choices make a difference.

Cape Town is at the forefront of what's likely to be a new way of life in our increasingly overextended world. Experiences like these challenge our perceptions of what we need and of what's precious. You could think of it as practice for what's to come.

It rained lightly here last week, and I stared at it with the same awe with which I watched the recent solar eclipse. It shouldn't take a drought to cultivate respect for our natural resources and compel more sustainable lives. But that's where we are in Cape Town.

DIANNA KANE IS THE CHIEF DESIGN OFFICER OF THE NONPROFIT TECHNOLOGY COMPANY MEDIC MOBILE.

# A Spy's Guide to Climate Change

OPINION  |  BY JUSTIN GILLIS  |  FEB. 15, 2018

THE TRUMP ADMINISTRATION is seeking to withdraw the United States from the international accord reached in Paris in 2015 to fight climate change. It is trying to rescind regulations on the issue. It has even scrubbed mentions of global warming from government websites. Yet its attempt to suppress the facts has not entirely succeeded, with federal agencies continuing to issue warnings, including in a major climate report published last year.

The latest climate alarm came this week in a Worldwide Threat Assessment of the U.S. Intelligence Community. Here is what the document, issued by Daniel R. Coats, the director of national intelligence, said about climate change and other environmental problems, with my annotations:

## A REAL PROBLEM

*The impacts of the long-term trends toward a warming climate, more air pollution, biodiversity loss, and water scarcity are likely to fuel economic and social discontent — and possibly upheaval — through 2018.*

Only six weeks into the year, this is already coming true. Cape Town, the second-largest city in South Africa, is so low on water after an extended drought that it may be forced to shut off the taps in early April. Water scarcity is a factor in the violent conflicts in Syria and Yemen, and in both countries, control of water supplies is being used as a weapon of war.

## SOCIAL DISRUPTIONS

*The past 115 years have been the warmest period in the history of modern civilization, and the past few years have been the warmest years on record. Extreme weather events in a warmer world have the potential for greater impacts and can compound with other drivers to raise the risk of humanitarian disasters, conflict, water and food shortages, population migration, labor shortfalls, price shocks, and power outages. Research has not identified indicators of tipping points in climate-linked Earth systems, suggesting a possibility of abrupt climate change.*

After running through an accurate summary of the warming trend and the risk it poses, the document appears — though the language is ambiguous — to suggest the possibility of sudden climate change of the sort that might cause global upheaval. Most scientists say that over the next few decades, at least, the likely prospect is a gradual worsening of climate-related problems.

But beyond a few decades, they are less willing to rule out catastrophes like the disappearance of polar sea ice, which could potentially cause profound climatic disruption.

## THREATS TO POLITICAL STABILITY

*Worsening air pollution from forest burning, agricultural waste incineration, urbanization, and rapid industrialization — with increasing public awareness — might drive protests against authorities , such as those recently in China, India, and Iran.*

The document does not explicitly mention the burning of fossil fuels, but that is a main cause of the poor air quality that plagues many cities in the developing world, and has even caused deteriorating air quality in places like London. Burning coal and oil not only causes climate change, it throws particles into the air that can cause asthma, heart attacks and other health problems. The World Health Organization estimates that three million people die prematurely every year because of outdoor air pollution, and over four million more because of indoor exposure to dirty fuels used for heating and cooking.

## CRITICAL SYSTEMS AT RISK

*Accelerating biodiversity and species loss — driven by pollution, warming, unsustainable fishing, and acidifying oceans — will jeopardize vital ecosystems that support critical human systems. Recent estimates suggest that the current extinction rate is 100 to 1,000 times the natural extinction rate.*

As the document implies, scientists are not entirely sure how much the rate of extinction has sped up because of human activities, but they do think it has accelerated. Some of them fear that we have entered the early stages of what will become the sixth mass extinction of organisms in Earth's history.

## CONFLICTS BETWEEN NATIONS

*Water scarcity, compounded by gaps in cooperative management agreements for nearly half of the world's international river basins, and new unilateral dam development are likely to heighten tension between countries.*

The biggest thing missing from this document is any explicit attribution of the cause of global climate disruption. Scientists have largely ruled out any natural explanation, concluding that the human release of greenhouse gases explains basically all the warming that has occurred since the 19th century. The two great culprits are the burning of fossil fuels and the chopping down of forests.

**JUSTIN GILLIS** IS A CONTRIBUTING OPINION WRITER.

# Planning for an Uncertain Future

The reality of climate change has become visible in many places, and the focus is now on how to prepare for more changes to come. Not only might people be forced to find new homes as climate refugees, but their behavior may have to change as well. Additionally, scientists are trying to predict which places will escape the worst effects, which ones may be impacted first and how to protect cities that are already in peril.

## Resettling the First American 'Climate Refugees'

**BY CORAL DAVENPORT AND CAMPBELL ROBERTSON  |  MAY 3, 2016**

ISLE DE JEAN CHARLES, LA. — Each morning at 3:30, when Joann Bourg leaves the mildewed and rusted house that her parents built on her grandfather's property, she worries that the bridge connecting this spit of waterlogged land to Louisiana's terra firma will again be flooded and she will miss another day's work.

Ms. Bourg, a custodian at a sporting goods store on the mainland, lives with her two sisters, 82-year-old mother, son and niece on land where her ancestors, members of the Native American tribes of southeastern Louisiana, have lived for generations. That earth is now dying, drowning in salt and sinking into the sea, and she is ready to leave.

With a first-of-its-kind "climate resilience" grant to resettle the island's native residents, Washington is ready to help.

"Yes, this is our grandpa's land," Ms. Bourg said. "But it's going under one way or another."

In January, the Department of Housing and Urban Development announced grants totaling $1 billion in 13 states to help communities adapt to climate change, by building stronger levees, dams and drainage systems.

One of those grants, $48 million for Isle de Jean Charles, is something new: the first allocation of federal tax dollars to move an entire community struggling with the impacts of climate change. The divisions the effort has exposed and the logistical and moral dilemmas it has presented point up in microcosm the massive problems the world could face in the coming decades as it confronts a new category of displaced people who have become known as climate refugees.

"We're going to lose all our heritage, all our culture," lamented Chief Albert Naquin of the Biloxi-Chitimacha-Choctaw, the tribe to which most Isle de Jean Charles residents belong. "It's all going to be history."

Around the globe, governments are confronting the reality that as human-caused climate change warms the planet, rising sea levels, stronger storms, increased flooding, harsher droughts and dwindling freshwater supplies could drive the world's most vulnerable people from their homes. Between 50 million and 200 million people — mainly subsistence farmers and fishermen — could be displaced by 2050 because of climate change, according to estimates by the United Nations University Institute for Environment and Human Security and the International Organization for Migration.

"The changes are underway and they are very rapid," Interior Secretary Sally Jewell warned last week in Ottawa. "We will have climate refugees."

But the problem is complex, said Walter Kaelin, the head of the Nansen Initiative, a research organization working with the United Nations to address extreme-weather displacement.

"You don't want to wait until people have lost their homes, until they flee and become refugees," he said. "The idea is to plan ahead and provide people with some measure of choice."

The Isle de Jean Charles resettlement plan is one of the first programs of its kind in the world, a test of how to respond to climate change in the most dramatic circumstances without tearing communities apart. Under the terms of the federal grant, the island's residents are to be resettled to drier land and a community that as of now does not exist. All funds have to be spent by 2022.

"We see this as setting a precedent for the rest of the country, the rest of the world," said Marion McFadden, who is running the program at the Department of Housing and Urban Development.

But even a plan like this — which would move only about 60 people — has been hard to pull off. Three previous resettlement efforts dating back to 2002 failed after they became mired in logistical and political complications. The current plan faces all the same challenges, illustrating the limitations of resettlement on any larger scale.

For over a century, the American Indians on the island fished, hunted, trapped and farmed among the lush banana and pecan trees that once spread out for acres. But since 1955, more than 90 percent of the island's original land mass has washed away. Channels cut by loggers and oil companies eroded much of the island, and decades of flood control efforts have kept once free-flowing rivers from replenishing the wetlands' sediments. Some of the island was swept away by hurricanes.

What little remains will eventually be inundated as burning fossil fuels melt polar ice sheets and drive up sea levels, projected the National Climate Assessment, a report of 13 federal agencies that highlighted the Isle de Jean Charles and its tribal residents as among the nation's most vulnerable.

Already, the homes and trailers bear the mildewed, rusting scars of increasing floods. The fruit trees are mostly gone or dying thanks to saltwater in the soil. Few animals are left to hunt or trap.

Violet Handon Parfait sees nothing but a bleak future in the rising waters. She lives with her husband and two children in a small trailer behind the wreckage of their house, which Hurricane Gustav destroyed in 2008.

The floods ruined the trailer's oven, so the family cooks on a hot plate. Water destroyed the family computer, too. Ms. Parfait, who has lupus, is afraid of what will happen if she is sick and cannot reach a doctor over the flooded bridge.

Ms. Parfait, who dropped out of high school, hopes for a brighter future, including college, for her children, Heather, 15, and Reggie, 13. But the children often miss school when flooding blocks their school bus.

"I just want to get out of here," she said.

Still, many residents of Isle de Jean Charles do not want to leave. Attachment to the island runs deep. Parents and grandparents lived here; there is a cemetery on the island that no one wants to abandon. Old and well-earned distrust of the government hangs over all efforts, and a bitter dispute between the two Indian tribes with members on the island has thwarted efforts to unite behind a plan.

"Ain't nobody I talk to that wants to move," said Edison Dardar, 66, a lifelong resident who has erected handwritten signs at the entrance to the island declaring his refusal to leave. "I don't know who's in charge of all this."

Whether to leave is only the first of the hard questions: Where does everyone go? What claim do they have to what is left behind? Will they be welcomed by their new neighbors? Will there be work nearby? Who will be allowed to join them?

"This is not just a simple matter of writing a check and moving happily to a place where they are embraced by their new neighbors," said Mark Davis, the director of the Tulane Institute on Water Resources Law and Policy.

"If you have a hard time moving dozens of people," he continued, "it becomes impossible in any kind of organized or fair way to move thousands, or hundreds of thousands, or, if you look at the forecast for South Florida, maybe even millions."

Louisiana officials have been coping with some of the fastest rates of land loss in the world — an area the size of Delaware has disappeared from south Louisiana since the 1930s. A master plan that is expected to cost tens of billions of dollars envisions a giant wall of levees and flood walls along the coast.

But some places, like the island, would be left on the outside. For those communities, wholesale relocation may be an effective tool, if a far more difficult and costly one.

"That's one of the things we need to learn from the creation of this model, which is how to do it economically," said Pat Forbes, the executive director of the state's Office of Community Development, the agency in charge of administering the federal climate grant.

A vast majority of the $1 billion disaster-resilience grant program is spent on projects to improve infrastructure, like stronger roads, bridges, dams, levees and drainage systems, to withstand rising seas and stronger storms.

But experts see places like Isle de Jean Charles as lost causes.

"We are very cognizant of the obligation to taxpayers to not throw good money after bad," Ms. McFadden of the Department of Housing and Urban Development said. "We could give the money to the island to build back exactly as before, but we know from the climate data that they will keep getting hit with worse storms and floods, and the taxpayer will keep getting hit with the bill."

With door-to-door visits, the state is only beginning to find out what the residents want in a new plan, Mr. Forbes said.

The location of the new community has not been chosen. Chiefs of the two tribes present on the island — the Biloxi-Chitimacha-Choctaw and the United Houma Nation — have debated who would be allowed to live there beyond the islanders themselves, and whether some islanders could resettle elsewhere. One of the planners involved in the resettlement suggested a buffer area between the new community and its surrounding neighborhood to reduce tension. Chief Naquin wants a live buffalo on site.

What has been decided, and what was essential for the islanders' support, is that the move be voluntary.

"I've lived my whole life here, and I'm going to die here," said Hilton Chaisson, who raised 10 sons on the island and wants his 26 grandchildren to know the same life of living off the land.

He conceded that the flooding has worsened, but, he said, "we always find a way."

# Where Can You Escape the Harshest Effects of Climate Change?

BY JONAH ENGEL BROMWICH | OCT. 20, 2016

It's hard to imagine that any city in North America will escape the effects of climate change within the next 25 years.

But some will be better positioned than others to escape the brunt of "drought, wildfire, extreme heat, extreme precipitation, extreme weather and hurricanes."

Those were some of the climate change-related threats listed by Benjamin Strauss, who focuses on climate impacts at Climate Central, an independent nonprofit research collaboration of scientists and journalists.

Dr. Strauss, 44, identified cities where people could settle in the next two decades if they are aiming to avoid those threats.

"Cities are certainly all going to be livable over the next 25 years, but they'll be increasingly feeling the heat," Dr. Strauss said, adding that political action could help cities mitigate the effects of climate change.

I also spoke with David W. Titley, 58, a professor of meteorology at Penn State University, and Katharine Hayhoe, 44, a professor of political science at Texas Tech University who works with cities to build resilience to climate risks.

Just because a city isn't mentioned within this piece does not mean it is not a good bet. My advice: If you're looking for a place to live, pay attention to the qualities of the cities more than the specific locations.

All three emphasized that while certain cities were better bets, their safety was relative.

"I don't care if you found the safest place in the U.S.," Dr. Titley said. "We're all going to pay, we're all going to suffer that economic disruption, we're all going to pay for that relocation."

## PORTLAND, ME.

My gut feeling before I talked to the scientists was that landlocked cities would be safer than those on the coasts. But Dr. Strauss set me straight.

"I don't think that I would restrict myself to only landlocked cities," he said. "There certainly are some coastal cities that are better positioned to weather rising seas than others."

One, he said, is Portland, which is well situated in the north and has a hilly topography.

Dr. Titley agreed that Portland was a solid option.

"Portland is high enough that certainly for the next few centuries it is not going to have significant sea-level rise," he said. "In general, cities north of 40 degrees latitude are not going to have the same type of systemic drought issues as cities further to the south."

## A MIDWESTERN TRIFECTA: DETROIT, CHICAGO AND MADISON, WIS.

Cities near the Great Lakes are reasonable options, all three scientists said.

"That region is probably one of the safest from a climate perspective," Dr. Strauss said.

"The Northeast and Midwest are going to have plenty of water, and they're not going to be subject to coastal flood issues," he said. "The Great Lakes are very much an advantage as a water supply."

He said that Midwestern cities would have to invest in more air-conditioning and would probably experience more extreme rainfall than other regions. But he said that they would not see the "dangerous heat that we'll be seeing in the southwest and the southeast."

But Dr. Hayhoe said that in the Midwestern cities, particularly Chicago, flooding will be a risk, saying that there had been a nearly 45 percent increase in heavy precipitation events in the Midwest since the 1950s.

## SAN FRANCISCO

Dr. Strauss was bullish on San Francisco and other cities along the northwest coast, saying that they would be insulated against "miserable hot weather" and wouldn't have much of a problem with sea level rise.

Dr. Titley said he was a "little less sanguine about the West Coast as a place to 'escape climate change.'"

He said that San Francisco, which already struggles with economic inequality, would be far more welcoming to those in a better position financially.

"People with resources have more adaptive capability," he said. "So the people with fewer resources are the ones that, unless we have a system to take care of them, are going to suffer disproportional impacts."

"That is a very legitimate policy and political decision," he said, "as opposed to the silliness of arguing whether climate change is happening."

## BOISE, IDAHO

Dr. Titley said Boise might be a safer bet than some of the West Coast cities.

But he also warned of wildfires in the Boise region, adding that the city itself was likely safer from that risk.

"If somebody pointed a gun at me and said, 'Boise or Denver, choose one on a climate-related basis,' I would choose Boise," he said. "That would be pretty easy."

Dr. Strauss agreed that from a climate perspective, Boise outranked Denver and other Southwestern cities like Tucson and Phoenix.

"The drought risk is lower, the heat risk is lower," he said.

Forest fires don't often affect large cities directly, but they do affect air quality, something that Dr. Strauss said was "not to be understated as an issue."

## NEW YORK CITY

Perhaps the biggest surprise to me during my conversations with the scientists was their general enthusiasm for New York City. Dr. Strauss and Dr. Titley said the city seemed serious about evaluating the risks of climate change.

Dr. Strauss mentioned a comprehensive environmental program, PlaNYC, proposed by Mayor Michael R. Bloomberg in 2007, and said that the administration of Mayor Bill de Blasio had embraced that path.

"New York City has some landscape advantages and has some landscape challenges," he said. "But it also has a lot of resources and is beginning to invest in preparing for higher seas. It has a long way to go, but it recognizes that and is beginning the journey."

Dr. Titley said the city would remain relatively safe from climate change except in the lowest-lying areas, like Lower Manhattan.

"I would argue that the governance in New York City has been more progressive than in many places on this issue," he said.

## STATE COLLEGE, PA.

Dr. Titley recommended State College, which is home to Pennsylvania State University. He said that the city's climate resistance was a consideration when he and his wife moved there three years ago.

"Our average temperatures, in the summertime, we'll get maybe a few days above 90 degrees," he said. "Our winter times are mild compared to New York State and New England. We'll probably be O.K. with water."

## TORONTO

Dr. Hayhoe said Toronto's developed infrastructure, financial system and public services were not likely to be affected by rising sea levels or water shortages.

And she made a final point about cities' vulnerability to climate change.

"Two-thirds of the world's biggest cities are within a few feet of sea level," she said. "If sea level were rising a thousand years ago, when people lived in tents, then if you lived in Houston, New

Orleans, New York, Mumbai or Shanghai, you'd pick up your tents and you'd move.

She pointed out that many of the seven and a half billion people on earth "are living in an increasingly urbanized environment within reach of the sea level rise that will occur this century. That is one of the biggest reasons we care about a changing climate."

# The Real Unknown of Climate Change: Our Behavior

BY JUSTIN GILLIS  |  SEPT. 18, 2017

AS HURRICANE HARVEY bore down on the Texas coast, few people in that state seemed to understand the nature of the looming danger.

The bulletins warned of rain falling in feet, not inches. Experts pleaded with the public to wake up. J. Marshall Shepherd, head of atmospheric sciences at the University of Georgia and a leading voice in American meteorology, wrote ahead of the storm that "the most dangerous aspect of this hurricane may be days of rainfall and associated flooding."

Now we know how events in Texas turned out.

Dr. Shepherd and his colleagues have spent their careers issuing a larger warning, one that much of the public still chooses to ignore. I speak, of course, about the risks of climate change.

ERIC THAYER FOR THE NEW YORK TIMES

Receding floodwaters from Hurricane Harvey in Port Arthur, Tex. Urgent warnings from meteorologists of the hurricane's dangers went unheeded by many.

Because of atmospheric emissions from human activity, the ocean waters from which Harvey drew its final burst of strength were much warmer than they ought to have been, most likely contributing to the intensity of the deluge. If the forecasts from our scientists are anywhere close to right, we have seen nothing yet.

In their estimation, the most savage heat waves that we experience today will likely become routine in a matter of decades. The coastal inundation that has already begun will grow worse and worse, forcing millions of people to flee. The immense wave of refugees that we already see moving across continents may be just the beginning.

Scientists urged decades ago that we buy ourselves some insurance by cutting emissions. We yawned. Even today, when millions of people have awakened to the danger, tens of millions have not. So the political demand for change is still too weak to overcome the entrenched interests that want to block it.

In Washington, progress on climate change has stalled. The administration has announced its intent to withdraw from the global Paris climate accord. And top Trump appointees insist that the causes of climate change are too uncertain and the scientific forecasts too unreliable to be a basis for action.

This argument might have been halfway plausible 20 years ago — or, if you want to be generous, even 10 years ago. But today?

Today, salt water is inundating the coastal towns of the United States, to the point that they are starting to put giant rulers in the intersections so people can tell if it is safe to drive through. The city leaders are also posting "no wake" signs not on canals but on the streets, to stop trucks from plowing through the water so fast as to send waves crashing into nearby homes.

We all see the giant storms, more threatening than any in our lifetimes — and while scientists are not entirely comfortable yet drawing links between the power of these hurricanes and climate change, many people are coming to their own common-sense conclusions.

Scott Pruitt, head of the Environmental Protection Agency.

As the challenges in the real world worsen, some senior Republicans continue to question the link between human-caused emissions and rising temperatures. Scott Pruitt, the head of the Environmental Protection Agency, said this on CNBC in March:

*I think that measuring with precision human activity on the climate is something very challenging to do and there's tremendous disagreement about the degree of impact, so no, I would not agree that it's a primary contributor to the global warming that we see.*

Note that he acknowledges the planet is warming. Note that he offers no alternative hypothesis about the cause of that warming — nor will he ever, for the simple reason that there is no plausible alternative. But still, he clings to uncertainty as a reason to do nothing.

To be sure, fair-minded people can and should ask: What are the real uncertainties?

They exist in climate science, and despite claims to the contrary made by climate denialists, nobody hides them. You can spend long days at conferences, as I have, hearing from the scientists themselves about all the error bars of their studies and all the weak points of their computer models.

We are not entirely sure, for instance, how much the planet will warm in response to a given level of emissions. That is a pretty basic question, and the inability of climate science to narrow it down has been one of the great frustrations of the field these past few decades.

In the 1970s, the experts made a best guess about how sensitive the Earth would be to greenhouse gases, and as evidence accumulates, that early estimate is holding up pretty well. Forecasts from the 1980s and 1990s about the rate of warming have proven fairly accurate, too, give or take 20 percent.

In fact, to the degree our scientists have made a systematic error, it has been to understate how quickly things would unravel.

The sea ice in the Arctic is collapsing in front of our eyes. Even more ominously, land ice is melting at an accelerating pace, threatening a future rise of the sea even faster than that of today.

Huge forest die-offs are beginning, even as the remaining forests work overtime to suck up some of the carbon pollution that humans are pumping out. We are already seeing heat waves surpassing 120 degrees Fahrenheit, sooner than many experts thought likely.

Yet, it is true, the list of uncertainties is still long and vexing. Scientists have trouble, for instance, turning their broad global forecasts into specific predictions for a given locality.

Want to know what the average temperature is going to be in Athens, Ga., in 2050? Wonder how the Asian monsoon, whose rains feed billions, will hold up in the 2070s? Those forecasts exist, but even the scientists who made them are not going to advise you to put much stock in them.

Yet here is the crucial point, and one you never hear the climate denialists own up to: the uncertainties cut in both directions.

Every time some politician stands up and claims that climate science is rife with uncertainties, a more honest person would add that those uncertainties could just as easily go against us as in our favor.

And if they do go against us? We might be looking at, oh, 80 or 100 feet of sea-level rise in the long haul, a direct result of the failures of this generation to get emissions under control. What kind of shape do you think Miami — or for that matter, New York — is likely to be in after 80 feet of sea-level rise?

The truth is that the single biggest uncertainty in climate science has nothing to do with the physics of the atmosphere, or the stability of the ice, or anything like that. The great uncertainty is, and has always been, how much carbon pollution humans are going to choose to pump into the air.

In fact, calculations have been run on this. If you want, say, a forecast for global temperature in 2100, the uncertainty about how much pollution we will spew out is at least twice as large as any uncertainty about the physical response of the climate to those emissions.

So despite arguments like Mr. Pruitt's, a century of climate science has brought us to the point where we can say this definitively: We are running enormous risks. We are putting nothing less than the stability of human civilization on the line.

And yet most of us have still not bestirred ourselves to care, much less to march in the streets demanding change. We are like the people in Texas who did not take those flood warnings seriously enough, except that the stakes are so much larger.

Is this failure to act the legacy our generation wants to leave for the generations yet to come?

# Of 21 Winter Olympic Cities, Many May Soon Be Too Warm to Host the Games

BY KENDRA PIERRE-LOUIS AND NADJA POPOVICH | JAN. 11, 2018

DISTILL THE UPCOMING Winter Olympics in Pyeongchang, South Korea, to their essence and you get 15 sports that involve gliding on snow or ice. Because of climate change, though, by 2050 many prior Winter Games locations may be too warm to ever host the Games again.

A team of researchers, led by Daniel Scott, a geography professor at the University of Waterloo in Ontario, came to that conclusion by taking climate data from previous Winter Games locations and applying climate-change models to predict future winter weather conditions.

The research, originally published in 2014, was updated this month to include the Pyeongchang Olympics, which begin Feb. 9, and the 2022 Winter Games in Beijing.

According to Dr. Scott's research, using emissions projections in which global greenhouse gas emissions continue to rise through mid-century and global temperatures increase by 4 degrees Fahrenheit by 2050, nine of the host locations will be too hot to handle the Games. But that temperature increase won't be felt equally. Chamonix, France, the site of the first Winter Games, will have winter temperatures 5.4 degrees Fahrenheit warmer by midcentury.

Dr. Scott's model factors in artificial snowmaking, but that has its limits. The technology involves pumping water through small nozzles under high pressure. When the water hits cold air it freezes almost instantly and turns into snow — but only if the air is cold enough.

"You're relying on cold air to do the refrigeration for you," Dr. Scott said. When the temperatures are above freezing, as they were during the 2010 Winter Games in Vancouver and the 2014 Winter Games in Sochi, you have to turn to more extreme measures.

In Vancouver, which melted under one of its warmest winters on record, organizers brought in 1,000 bales of straw and covered them with a mix of artificial snow and natural snow hauled in from higher elevations to cover the bare ski slopes.

When shortages of cold and snow are combined, four former venues are likely to be unreliable hosts by midcentury. Five more will be risky.

In Sochi, whose mild climate made it an unusual choice for the Winter Games, organizers banked snow from the previous winter, storing it in shady places and covering it with insulation.

Both locations also used technology that involves embedding pipes with dry ice in the sites for aerials and moguls skiing. The technique supposedly preserves snow for up to two days by cooling it from the bottom up.

Despite these efforts, athletes at both Games complained of poor snow that they said led to unfair conditions.

Skiers, for example, may consider a competition unfair when shifting conditions make a course faster or slower depending on when the skier races. At Sochi, snowboarders complained that the half-pipe was dangerous because of bumps and sugary snow that can slow down riders when they should be gaining speed for maneuvers that involve launching as much as 20 feet above the half-pipe's 22-foot top edge. During the event's qualifying runs, more than half of the athletes fell.

In the past, Olympic organizers have dealt with the vagaries of weather by bringing events indoors. Skating events were once held outside, for instance. But you can't move the mountains required for the giant slalom or the 50-kilometer course for one of the men's cross country ski events indoors.

Even in a warming world, some regions will still have cold places. But the number of possible Winter Olympics locations will decline. In the future, the Winter Games might rotate through a handful of the same cities.

At the same time, the warming climate affects not only the locations of the Olympics, but also the ability of athletes to train. In the

United States, some ski locations are forecast to see seasons 50 percent shorter by 2050 and 80 percent shorter by 2090.

That will complicate life for elite athletes, but they can at least travel to find snow.

The repercussions are potentially much more serious for young athletes getting a first taste of winter sports. What will happen to the pipeline that feeds elite sports programs when the local ski hill, or the frozen pond where kids play hockey, disappears?

"It's an interesting question that nobody really knows the answer to," Dr. Scott said.

# Fortified but Still in Peril, New Orleans Braces for Its Future

BY JOHN SCHWARTZ AND MARK SCHLEIFSTEIN | FEB. 24, 2018

In the years after Hurricane Katrina, over 350 miles of levees, flood walls, gates and pumps came to encircle greater New Orleans. Experts say that is not enough.

NEW ORLEANS — Burnell Cotlon lost everything in Hurricane Katrina — "just like everyone else," he said.

When the flawed flood wall bordering his neighborhood here in the Lower Ninth Ward gave way in August 2005, the waters burst through with explosive force that pushed his home off its foundations and down the street. What was left: rubble, mud and mold.

Not far from his rebuilt home stands a rebuilt flood wall, taller

WILLIAM WIDMER FOR THE NEW YORK TIMES

The West Closure Complex is part of a sprawling hurricane risk reduction system that protects greater New Orleans. The city is visible in the distance.

and more solidly anchored in its levee than the old one. On the other side of that lies the canal whose storm-swollen waters toppled the old wall, letting Lake Pontchartrain spill into the neighborhood and then sit, more than 10 feet deep, for weeks on end. As an added shield, an enormous gate closes the canal off from the lake when storms approach. Similar gates can secure the city's other major canals. In all, federal, state and local governments spent more than $20 billion on the 350 miles of levees, flood walls, gates and pumps that now encircle greater New Orleans.

"I hope and pray that the money was well spent and it is a decent system," said Mr. Cotlon, who opened the first grocery store in the still-recovering neighborhood in 2014.

This year, New Orleans celebrates its 300th birthday. Whether it will see 400 is no sure thing.

As Jean Lafitte and other vulnerable little towns that fringe the bayous plead for some small measure of salvation, New Orleans today

WILLIAM WIDMER FOR THE NEW YORK TIMES

During Katrina in 2005, floodwaters pushed Burnell Cotlon's home off its foundations and down the street in the Lower Ninth Ward.

is a fortress city, equipped with the best environmental protection it has ever had — probably the strongest, in fact, that any American city has ever had. Yet even the system's creators have conceded that it may not be strong enough.

The problem, in the argot of flood protection, is that the Army Corps of Engineers designed the new system to protect against the storms that would cause a "100-year" flood — a flood with a 1 percent chance of occurring in any given year. And that, experts say, is simply insufficient for an urban area certain to face more powerful storms.

"All along we knew that 100-year was somewhat voodoo math," said Garret Graves, a Republican congressman from Louisiana and former chairman of the state's Coastal Protection and Restoration Authority. Indeed, the corps has stopped calling its handiwork a hurricane protection system, opting instead for the more modest Hurricane & Storm Damage Risk Reduction System.

How that came to be is a story of money and politics and, perhaps, a degree of Louisiana fatalism. In simplest terms, though, it comes down to a mismatch between limited resources and limitless amounts of water.

If New Orleans is culturally and culinarily unique among American cities, it is also uniquely vulnerable: Half the city lies below sea level, and is sinking still, and the buffer of protective wetlands that can knock down the force of incoming hurricanes is eroding away.

Climate change threatens to make these problems far worse. The rising oceans will strengthen storm surges, and increased moisture in the atmosphere will add to the drenching rains that regularly overwhelm the city's aging drainage system. Scientists also suggest that a warming world will bring stronger hurricanes.

"Climate change is turning that 100-year flood, that 1 percent flood, into a 5 percent flood or a 20-year flood," said Rick Luettich, a storm surge expert and vice chairman of one of the New Orleans area's two regional levee authorities. By that inexorable logic, the 500-year flood becomes a 100-year flood, and so on.

VINCENT LAFORET/THE NEW YORK TIMES

Katrina's floodwaters overwhelmed a levee in the Industrial Canal and spilled into the Lower Ninth Ward.

The corps itself has repeatedly acknowledged that the new system will not prevent future floods. "There's still going to be a lot of people that will be inundated," the corps's former commander, the retired Lt. Gen. Robert L. Van Antwerp, warned as far back as 2009. In storms at 200- to 500-year levels, the corps has said, New Orleans could still suffer breaches like those experienced during Katrina.

As he ends his eight-year run at City Hall, the mayor, Mitch Landrieu, sounds as if he has a bit of the prophet about him. The combination of sea level rise, subsidence and coastal erosion, he said in an interview, poses an "existential threat" for New Orleans.

"What we should have done," Mr. Landrieu said, "is build to a 10,000-year flood standard, which is what the Netherlands built to, and we didn't, and that was for the country a monetary decision."

Now, he fears, his city itself could join a variety of landmarks that, as a popular local song puts it, "ain't dere no more."

## A DEVIL'S BARGAIN

The Army Corps spent nearly 50 years building the old hurricane protection system for New Orleans. More than 1,400 people died in the city when it failed. So in the aftermath of Katrina, Congress thought big.

Funding measures that passed beginning in late 2005 outlined a three-stage program for restoring a shattered and sodden New Orleans. The first step was to repair the broken levees and flood walls to what they were before the storm. At the same time, the corps would develop a plan to offer "interim protection," that 100-year level, achievable within several years. Finally, Congress called on the secretary of the Army, who oversees the corps, to "consider providing protection for a storm surge equivalent to a Category 5 hurricane — a storm, that is, more powerful than Katrina."

A range of experts consulted by the corps called for defense of that level or higher. Indeed, a study by Dutch engineers found that central New Orleans needed protection against the kind of storm that might show up once in 5,000 years.

In the end, though, the interim level became the benchmark. One central factor was a congressional compromise reached during the George W. Bush administration that came to be known locally as the Devil's bargain. Under the deal, New Orleanians would remain eligible for federal flood insurance if the system could be brought up to the 100-year level — the protection needed for insurance eligibility in what the government defines as a flood zone. An insurance standard became a proxy for a safety standard.

Though the corps produced a 4,000-page report with a host of alternatives, it offered no recommended course of action. That, along with the financing, largely fell to the state. By 2012, the state's Coastal Protection and Restoration Authority had already issued two versions of its own master plan, the later one calling for Katrina-level or greater protection for New Orleans. But when the third plan was released in 2017, predictions for the effects of climate change had outstripped ambition: The seas were rising so fast, the authors concluded, that with its $50 billion price tag for greater New Orleans and the south Louisiana coast, the hoped-for protection was out of reach. What's more, that much money might never become available.

Sidney Coffee, who led the state authority from 2005 to 2008, said the state had to balance the needs of the city with those of the rest of Louisiana. "The state has always wanted the best, the highest level of protection that could be afforded for New Orleans," she said.

Knowing that the new flood walls and earthen levees weren't high enough to stop a Katrina-like surge, the corps built in features intended to keep them standing, including erosion-fighting measures like concrete "splash pads" to prevent overflow from washing away supporting soil. Deeper pilings will help the walls stay upright. Gates to keep Lake Pontchartrain from pouring in should mean less water to pump out after a storm.

Because of measures like these, "what resulted from the design was much more like a 500-year system than a 100-year system," said Ed Link, an engineering professor at the University of Maryland who led the corps-sponsored investigation of the levee failures in Katrina. With an emphasis on improving evacuation protocols, even supplying transportation for pets, fewer deaths are expected during the next Katrina.

But the flooding could still be severe — during a 500-year flood, as much as five feet deep in the half of the city that sits below sea level. In August, a thunderstorm dumped between six and nine inches of rain over parts of the city within a three-hour period, overwhelming antiquated pumps — some dating to 1912 — and causing extensive flooding. Updating the drainage system will cost at least $1 billion through 2026, and perhaps much more.

## CHALLENGES AHEAD

One of the most spectacular features of the city's new defenses is a 1.8-mile-long wall that cuts across wetlands at a corner of Lake

A major part of the city's new defense system is the Lake Borgne Surge Barrier.

Borgne, east of the city. It stands 26 feet above the water line and cost $1.1 billion. Its support piles reach more than 100 feet into the muck of the lake. Its top is crenelated like a castle wall.

And it illustrates how, in many parts of New Orleans, upgrading further is not feasible.

The wall was designed for a 100-year storm, with some extra height to compensate for subsidence and estimated sea level rise over 50 years. But at this location, Katrina sent a far stronger surge.

There is no easy fix. While earthen levees can be raised by adding dirt, raising the wall even higher would be impractical, said Robert Turner, director of engineering and operations for the regional levee authority that operates the barrier. A cap of an additional foot could be built, he said, but "if you try to go higher than that over time, you can stress the pile foundations that hold this barrier in place."

To many local officials, 500-year protection is a fantasy. Susan Maclay, the head of the levee authority for the New Orleans-area communities on the west bank of the Mississippi River, said that finding the money to maintain the current system was daunting. The financially squeezed state government, too, is searching for a way to pay its share of the hurricane protection system — $100 million a year for the next 30.

"You're so focused on killing the snakes right in front of you that you can't, it's just not feasible, to think beyond the immediate problem," Ms. Maclay said.All the while, the rest of the state is waiting for its own 100-year protection.

"It's difficult to sell, on the state level, elevating New Orleans protection to 500 when you have places such as Jean Lafitte, Terrebonne Parish, Houma, New Iberia and other places that have zero level of protection, or at best 10-year protection," said Jerome Zeringue, a state representative. New Orleanians, he said, "should lessen their expectations."

The rest of the nation, too, awaits a higher level of protection from the effects of climate change: Major cities like New York and Miami, but also smaller communities like Galveston, Tex., want costly projects of their own. "The rest of the coast, and the rest of the country, needs help," said Col. Michael Clancy, commander of the New Orleans district of the corps.

Still, more must be done, said Mr. Graves, the Louisiana congressman. The projects to protect the state so far are tremendous, but what is to come will have to be "tremendouser," he said, adding, "People say we can't afford to do this — I would say we can't afford not to."

Repairing hurricane damage is always far more expensive than providing protection. Katrina cost between $120 billion and $150 billion, Mr. Graves noted. The new system has already saved hundreds of millions of dollars in smaller storms like Hurricane Isaac in 2012. "When a big one comes," he said, "that project will pay off multiple times over."

New Orleans residents like Artie Folse hope that is true. But Mr. Folse is also wary. His house near Lake Pontchartrain had to be rebuilt from the studs up after Katrina. If the next storm overwhelms the city's defenses, he said, "I can't do it again."

# Providing for 7 Billion. Or Not.

BY JOHN SCHWARTZ  |  FEB. 14, 2018

CAN WE PROVIDE good lives for the seven billion people on Earth without wrecking the planet?

Daniel O'Neill of the University of Leeds and colleagues asked this enormous question in a recent paper in the journal Nature Sustainability and on an accompanying website.

Their answer is uncomfortable. After looking at data on quality of life and use of resources from some 150 countries, they found that no nation currently meets the basic needs of its citizens in a sustainable way. The nations of the world either don't provide the basics of a good life or they do it at excessive cost in resources, or they fail at both.

To Dr. O'Neill, an economist, this was something of a surprise. "When we started, we kind of thought, 'surely, out of 150 different countries, there will be some shining star' " with a high quality of life and moderate resource use. "We really didn't find that," he said, pointing only to Vietnam as coming close to meeting both measures.

The United States, on the other hand, provides a relatively high quality of life but fails on every measure of sustainability in the study. For example, it emits 21.2 metric tons of carbon dioxide per person per year, while the study's sustainability threshold is 1.6 metric tons.

Providing a good quality of life to everyone on the planet would require "two to six times the sustainable level for resources," Dr. O'Neill said. "Something has to change."

He did not say, however, that these findings doom humanity to poverty or environmental ruin. "It doesn't tell us what's theoretically possible," he said, noting that the study only projects the results of continuing with business as usual.

The conclusions have caused a stir, especially in conservative circles. National Review denounced the paper as a call for "global wealth distribution," saying "the goal clearly is a technocracy that will undermine freedom, constrain opportunity, not truly benefit the poor, and materially harm societies that have moved beyond the struggle for survival."

Dr. O'Neill said that that reading of the paper missed the point — redistribution cannot solve the problem. Whoever owns the wealth, he said, "We need to improve both physical and social provisioning systems."

At the same time, global income inequality is an issue, he added wryly. "I am all for taking away yachts and providing food, clean water and access to electricity to people in sub-Saharan Africa."

# No Children Because of Climate Change? Some People Are Considering It

BY MAGGIE ASTOR  |  FEB. 5, 2018

ADD THIS to the list of decisions affected by climate change: Should I have children?

It is not an easy time for people to feel hopeful, with the effects of global warming no longer theoretical, projections becoming more dire and governmental action lagging. And while few, if any, studies have examined how large a role climate change plays in people's childbearing decisions, it loomed large in interviews with more than a dozen people ages 18 to 43.

A 32-year-old who always thought she would have children can no

JOSH HANER/THE NEW YORK TIMES

Rising waters are threatening low-lying areas like South Tarawa in Kiribati, a Pacific island nation.

longer justify it to herself. A Mormon has bucked the expectations of her religion by resolving to adopt rather than give birth. An Ohio woman had her first child after an unplanned pregnancy — and then had a second because she did not want her daughter to face an environmental collapse alone.

Among them, there is a sense of being saddled with painful ethical questions that previous generations did not have to confront. Some worry about the quality of life children born today will have as shorelines flood, wildfires rage and extreme weather becomes more common. Others are acutely aware that having a child is one of the costliest actions they can take environmentally.

The birthrate in the United States, which has been falling for a decade, reached a new low in 2016. Economic insecurity has been a major factor, but even as the economy recovers, the decline in births continues.

And the discussions about the role of climate change are only intensifying.

"When we first started this project, I didn't know anybody who had had any conversations about this," said Meghan Kallman, a co-founder of Conceivable Future, an organization that highlights how climate change is limiting reproductive choices.

That has changed, she said — either because more people are having doubts, or because it has become less taboo to talk about them.

## FACING AN UNCERTAIN FUTURE

If it weren't for climate change, Allison Guy said, she would go off birth control tomorrow.

But scientists' projections, if rapid action isn't taken, are not "congruent with a stable society," said Ms. Guy, 32, who works at a marine conservation nonprofit in Washington. "I don't want to give birth to a kid wondering if it's going to live in some kind of 'Mad Max' dystopia."

Parents like Amanda PerryMiller, a Christian youth leader and mother of two in Independence, Ohio, share her fears.

"Animals are disappearing. The oceans are full of plastic. The human population is so numerous, the planet may not be able to support it indefinitely," said Ms. PerryMiller, 29. "This doesn't paint a very pretty picture for people bringing home a brand-new baby from the hospital."

The people thinking about these issues fit no single profile. They are women and men, liberal and conservative. They come from many regions and religions.

Cate Mumford, 28, is a Mormon, and Mormons believe God has commanded them to "multiply and replenish the earth." But even in her teens, she said, she could not get another point of doctrine out of her head: "We are stewards of the earth."

Ms. Mumford, a graduate student in a joint-degree program at Johns Hopkins and Brigham Young Universities, plans to adopt a child with her husband. Some members of her church have responded aggressively, accusing her of going against God's plan. But she said she felt vindicated by the worsening projections.

A few years ago, she traveled to China, where air pollution is a national crisis. And all she could think was, "I'm so glad I'm not going to bring a brand-new baby into this world to suffer like these kids suffer."

### 'SOME PRETTY STRONG COGNITIVE DISSONANCE'

For many, the drive to reproduce is not easily put aside.

"If a family is what you want, you're not just going to be able to make that disappear entirely," said Jody Mullen, 36, a mother of two in Gillette, N.J. "You're not just going to be able to say, 'It's not really good for the environment for humans to keep reproducing, so I'll just scratch that idea.' "

And so compromises emerge. Some parents resolve to raise conscientious citizens who can help tackle climate change. Some who want multiple children decide to have only one.

For Sara Jackson Shumate, 37, who has a young daughter, having a second child would mean moving to a house farther from her job as a lecturer at the Metropolitan State University of Denver. She is not sure she can justify the environmental impact of a larger home and a longer commute.

But for Ms. PerryMiller, the Ohio youth leader, the thinking went the opposite way: Once she had her first child, climate change made a second feel more urgent.

"Someday, my husband and I will be gone," she said. "If my daughter has to face the end of the world as we know it, I want her to have her brother there."

Laura Cornish, 32, a mother of two near Vancouver, said she felt "some pretty strong cognitive dissonance around knowing that the science is really bad but still thinking that their future will be O.K."

"I don't read the science updates anymore because they're too awful," she said. "I just don't engage with that, because it's hard to reconcile with my choices."

## 'THE THING THAT'S BROKEN IS BIGGER THAN US'

People who choose not to have children are used to being called "selfish." But many of them see their decision as a sacrifice.

Parenthood is "something that I want," said Elizabeth Bogard, 18, a freshman at Northern Illinois University. "But it's hard for me to justify my wants over what matters and what's important for everyone."

This attitude seems particularly common among people who have seen the effects of climate change firsthand.

Hemanth Kolla is from Hyderabad, in India, where drought and scorching heat waves have been deadly. He lives in California, where the threat of wildfires is increasing and a six-year drought only recently ended. Mr. Kolla, 36, said it felt wrong to have a child when he did not believe the world would be better for him or her.

And Maram Kaff, who lives in Cairo, said she had been deeply affected by reports that parts of the Middle East may be too hot for human habitation by 2100.

"I've seen how Syrian refugees, who are running from a devastating war, are being treated," Ms. Kaff, 33, said in an email. "Imagine how my children will be treated if they have to flee their country due to extreme weather, drought, lack of resources, flooding."

"I know that humans are hard-wired to procreate," she said, "but my instinct now is to shield my children from the horrors of the future by not bringing them to the world."

Ms. Kallman and Josephine Ferorelli, the founders of Conceivable Future, said that the predominant emotion at their gatherings was grief — and that the very existence of these conversations should spur political action.

"These stories tell you that the thing that's broken is bigger than us," Ms. Ferorelli said. "The fact that people are seriously considering not having children because of climate change is all the reason you need to make the demands."

Most of the people interviewed, parents and non-parents alike, lamented having to factor climate change into their decisions at all.

"What kind of nightmare question is that?" asked Ms. Guy, the Washington nonprofit worker. "That we have to consider that?"

# What Land Will Be Underwater in 20 Years? Figuring It Out Could Be Lucrative

BY BRAD PLUMER | FEB. 23, 2018

IN CHARLESTON, S.C., where the ports have been expanding to accommodate larger ships sailing through the newly widened Panama Canal, a real-estate developer named Xebec Realty recently went looking for land to build new warehouses and logistics centers.

But first, Xebec had a question: What were the odds that the sites it was considering might be underwater in 10 or 20 years?

After all, Charleston has repeatedly suffered major floods that can paralyze cargo operations. And scientists warn that flooding will worsen as sea levels rise and storms strengthen with climate change.

Yet detailed information about the city's climate risks proved surprisingly hard to find. Federal flood maps are based on historical data, and won't tell you how sea-level rise could exacerbate flooding in the years ahead. Scientific reports on global warming, such as the National Climate Assessment, can tell you that heavy rainstorms are expected to increase in the Southeast, but they won't tell you whether specific roads leading to a given warehouse might be unusable during those storms.

So Xebec turned to a Silicon Valley start-up called Jupiter, which offered to analyze local weather and hydrological data and combine it with climate model projections to assess the potential climate risks Xebec might face in Charleston over the next few decades from things like heavier rainfall, sea level rise or increased storm surge.

Although Jupiter's forecasting skill remains unproven, Xebec was eager to participate in a pilot project. "If we could have reliable predictive analytics in this area, that's a huge impact for our business," said Scott Hodgkins, an executive vice president at Xebec.

As companies around the world grow concerned about the risks of climate change, they have started looking for clarity on how warming might disrupt their operations in the future. But governments in the United States and Europe have been slow to translate academic research on global warming into practical, timely advice for businesses or local city planners.

Now some private companies, like Jupiter, are trying to fill the gap.

This remains a young and untested field, and it's unclear whether Jupiter or others can succeed as profitable enterprises. Scientists caution that predicting short-term climate effects in specific locations remains rife with uncertainty. Jupiter will have to persuade potential customers that its forecasts are reliable enough to give companies a competitive edge.

"In economics, information has value if you would make a different decision based on that information," said Matthew E. Kahn, an economist who studies climate adaptation at the University of Southern California. "Is that the case here?"

Some insurance companies, such as FM Global, already study climate risks and consult with clients on how to make their buildings more resilient to hurricanes that may get stronger in the future. In 2014, a start-up called Coastal Risk Consulting opened in South Florida to offer flood assessments to homeowners nervous about rising seas.

Jupiter, founded in 2017 by Rich Sorkin, a longtime tech entrepreneur, wants to go a step further. The start-up has received $10 million in venture capital so far and has been hiring climate scientists, weather modelers and data experts from places like the National Oceanic and Atmospheric Administration. Its co-founders include Todd D. Stern, the lead climate envoy in the Obama administration, and Jeff Wecker, the chief data officer for Goldman Sachs.

The company is developing a variety of predictive tools, some of which look much like Google Maps, that it hopes will allow paying customers to zoom down to the city block level to get a better sense of the potential risks they face from storms, heat waves, wildfires or other climate-change effects in the coming decades.

"We know the planet's getting warmer and sea levels are rising, but on a hyperlocal basis, the quality of those predictions can be much better than it is," Mr. Sorkin said.

To create its flood maps, for instance, Jupiter looks not just at public data like satellite-based observations of rainfall and ocean currents, but also how changes in the urban landscape affect how water flows through cities. It then aims to harness recent advances in cloud-based supercomputing to combine that data with the latest climate model projections. The company's scientists plan to continually test their forecasts against observations — to see, for instance, how well they predict flooding from major storms — and publish their research in scientific journals.

In theory, the United States government could cobble much of this information together and present it in a usable way. But federal agencies tend to focus their resources on shorter-term weather predictions, and Congress has generally underfunded initiatives such as those at the Federal Emergency Management Agency to incorporate climate change into its federal flood maps.

"If you want a full picture of flooding risk, you need expertise in weather, but also climate and hydrology and engineering and running complex models on the latest computer hardware," Mr. Sorkin said. "All of those specialized disciplines are usually heavily siloed within the public sector or the scientific community."

Jupiter's scientists will have to grapple with a number of technical challenges. While current climate models can provide broad statistical projections of how average temperatures and rainfall patterns are likely to shift across large regions over the coming century, it remains difficult to predict such shifts precisely over shorter time scales — which is what companies are often most concerned about.

"Forecasting at 10-20 year time periods is perhaps the most difficult period to forecast," Simon Mason, a climate scientist at Columbia

University's International Research Institute for Climate and Society who is not involved with Jupiter, wrote in an email. "If that is not enough, trying to predict severe weather events rather than long-term averages is even harder still!"

Past efforts to provide what are known as "climate services" have struggled with this issue. In 2009, the German government established the Climate Service Center to provide information about global warming risks to cities and businesses. But Guy P. Brasseur, a climate scientist who helped start the center, said potential clients were often disappointed with the uncertainty in the resulting forecasts.

"One airline wanted to know how often the airport in Frankfurt would be closed because of snowstorms next year," Dr. Brasseur said. "We were unable to answer a question like that."

Jupiter, which acknowledges the uncertainties in climate forecasting, will have to prove that a market exists. But at least one firm in the insurance industry sees potential value in the company's approach, particularly after flooding and other disasters caused $306 billion in damages last year in the United States and record losses by insurers.

"That certainly raised the stakes in terms of trying to get the best possible science on your side when you're pricing risk," said John Drzik, president of global risk at Marsh, one of the world's largest commercial insurance brokers, which is currently in talks with Jupiter to explore what types of data and risk analyses might be most useful to its clients.

Mr. Drzik noted that many of the traditional catastrophic risk models used by the insurance industry are rooted largely in historical data and don't always grapple fully with how climate change could shift those risks in the future. While his company is still evaluating whether Jupiter's climate-oriented models are useful enough to be worth paying for, "it grabbed us as something that had a lot of promise."

As global warming advances, experts say that governments will ultimately have to invest more in their own local climate prediction tools to help cities and industries adapt. But they also see a role for private climate forecasters, much as weather companies have sprung up to supplement the work the National Weather Service does.

"The federal government could be doing a lot more," said James L. Buizer, who studies climate adaptation at the University of Arizona. "But there's still an important role for the private sector. If companies are going to benefit from this information, they ought to be paying for it. After all, it's their infrastructure that's going to get trashed."

# Forests Protect the Climate. A Future With More Storms Would Mean Trouble.

BY HENRY FOUNTAIN    |    MARCH 7, 2018

RIO GRANDE, P.R. — When Hurricane Maria walloped Puerto Rico in September, it ripped off roofs, flooded neighborhoods and all but destroyed the island's power grid, leaving a humanitarian catastrophe that Puerto Ricans are still recovering from months later.

But Maria took its toll on nature as well. Its winds of up to 155 miles an hour wrecked thousands of acres of trees, including much of El Yunque National Forest, 28,000 acres of lush tropical rain forest east of the capital, San Juan.

ERIKA P. RODRIGUEZ FOR THE NEW YORK TIMES

Volunteers getting instructions on how to assess damaged trees in El Yunque as part of a project led by María Uriarte, a Columbia University ecologist.

To a group of researchers hiking down a steep, slick mountain trail in El Yunque recently, the destruction was readily apparent. Led by María Uriarte, an ecologist at Columbia University, they were here to study the damage and better understand how an expected increase in extreme weather may undermine the ability of forests to aid the climate.

Before Maria, the mountainside here would have been in shade, a canopy of sierra palm fronds and leafy branches of yagrumo trees and others blocking much of the sunlight. But the winds knocked down many of the leafy trees, sheared off the branches of others and completely stripped the more flexible palms of their fronds. The slope was now open to the sky, and the outskirts of San Juan, normally blocked from view, were visible far in the distance.

Organized quickly after the hurricane, the research — starting with a painstaking, tree-by-tree damage assessment in representative plots — will analyze how severe storms affect the amount of carbon forests pull out of the atmosphere and store.

Dr. Uriarte.

And because climate change is expected to increase the frequency of extreme weather events in many parts of the world, the work will also help researchers understand how forests could be changed permanently as the world continues to warm.

"All the global climate models are predicting we're going to see more severe hurricanes," said Dr. Uriarte, who has studied the forests of Puerto Rico for a decade and a half. "So what does that mean for the composition of the forest?"

Trees are a critical part of the carbon cycle, in which carbon moves between the atmosphere, ocean and land. They remove atmospheric carbon dioxide, incorporating the carbon into their tissues as they grow. Worldwide, forests are a net storehouse, or sink, of carbon, removing one billion to two billion tons from the atmosphere each year. That's a substantial portion of the roughly 10 billion tons of carbon pumped into the air by fossil-fuel burning and other human activities.

When a forest is damaged, the dead vegetation eventually decomposes, returning the carbon to the atmosphere. The amount can be enormous: a study of damage after Hurricane Katrina in 2005 found that the storm killed or severely damaged 320 million trees across the Gulf Coast, containing about 100 million tons of carbon.

As forests start to recover, the mix of species is often different — in a rain forest like El Yunque, for example, species that thrive in full light tend to take over until the canopy regrows. The trees are also younger and smaller, so the recovering forest stores less carbon.

"Forests take a while to recover," said Louis Verchot, a researcher with the International Center for Tropical Agriculture in Palmira, Colombia. "And what initially recovers is not always what was there before."

If this cycle of damage and regrowth — what ecologists call a disturbance regime — occurs more often as extreme storms become more frequent, some forests may never recover completely. Over decades, the reduction in stored carbon would likely become permanent. More carbon from human activity would remain in the atmosphere to contribute to climate change, or would have to be removed in other ways.

A technician shows volunteers one way to measure the height of a damaged tree at a study plot in El Yunque.

"If the climate warms, do we expect an increase in disturbance regimes?" said Jeffrey Q. Chambers, a geographer at the University of California, Berkeley, who led the Katrina study. "That could work on the ability of those systems to remove $CO_2$ from the atmosphere."

Determining how the biomass in damaged forests changes over time is thus crucial to understanding the global carbon balance. But the work is not straightforward, as counting damaged trees in even a modest forest is a practical impossibility. Instead, researchers rely on remote sensing: satellite images to determine the presence or absence of trees, for example, or laser-based airborne measurements of a forest canopy.

### FOREST DAMAGE FROM HURRICANE MARIA

Using remote-sensing data, Dr. Chambers has come up with an estimate of the trees that were killed or severely damaged by Hurricane Maria in Puerto Rico: 23 million to 31 million.

Estimates like this are necessarily preliminary. For one thing, many trees may be alive now but will eventually die from storm damage; that was the case after Hurricane Katrina. The analyses also use software to interpret the data, so the results need to be validated by the basic scientific work of assessing the damage on the ground.

"You need ground data to make sure that what you're seeing makes sense," Dr. Uriarte said.

That's why she, three of her doctoral students and others were hiking down the mountain trail. Starting at about 3,000 feet elevation, near the highest point of El Yunque, their goal was to reach several study plots at intervals below.

The plots were established about two decades ago and have been studied over the years by scientists and staff at El Verde Field Station, a research outpost in the national forest that was built during the Cold War for United States government studies on the effects of radiation on vegetation.

In recent decades, with the radioactive contamination having been cleaned up, El Verde has been used for more benign research, including studies on the impact of climate change on tropical forests. Now operated by the University of Puerto Rico, the field station is home to one of the few long-term ecological monitoring programs in the tropics.

The descent was difficult, as the steep trail had been booby-trapped by downed trees and branches and covered with a thick layer of graying palm fronds.

"This is some extreme hiking," said Andrew Quebbeman, one of the students, who was hauling a high-precision GPS device.

The idea on this day was to use the GPS instrument, which is accurate to within four inches horizontally and vertically, to match an area on the ground to the same area on a Landsat satellite image of the forest.

By the standards of digital imaging, a Landsat image is extremely low resolution. It cannot make out individual trees. Instead, software

ERIKA P. RODRIGUEZ FOR THE NEW YORK TIMES

Andrew Quebbeman, a doctoral student with Dr. Uriarte's group, sets up a GPS instrument to determine a precise location in the damaged forest.

interprets the color in each small square of the image — each covering an area on the ground of about 100 feet by 100 feet — as intact or damaged forest, or bare ground.

By precisely locating one of these squares in the forest, the researchers could assess the actual condition of the trees within it and relate that to the color in the image. That will help improve the software and thus the estimates of damage across the island.

It helps that these plots, like others monitored by the field station, have been studied in the past. Each has been marked by corner stakes, and every tree with a trunk larger than about 4 inches in diameter has been identified and tagged, and its condition before the storm is known.

Once Mr. Quebbeman located the center of the square with the GPS instrument, the researchers divided the area into quarters and walked each one, stopping at each tree to assess its condition — noting whether each was alive or dead, standing or fallen, and, if a tree was damaged and standing, estimating how much of its canopy remained.

ERIKA P. RODRIGUEZ FOR THE NEW YORK TIMES

One of the project's study areas is a grid of 400 plots covering 40 acres. The orange measuring tapes are used to determine tree diameters.

Closer to El Verde, a group of eight volunteers — recent college graduates with an interest in natural science (and in living in Puerto Rico for six months) — were doing similar work at the field station's main study area, 40 acres of forest divided into a grid of 400 plots, each about 65 feet by 65 feet.

If anything, the damage was even worse there. Most of the palms were still standing, and in most cases two or three small fronds were already pushing out from their tops. But Maria had simply bowled over some of the other trees, leaving a jumbled mess of uprooted trunks that made it difficult to distinguish one from another. And there were so many dead palm fronds littering the ground that at times even finding the stakes marking each plot was a struggle.

While many areas were almost completely destroyed, others nearby seemed barely touched, depending on elevation, orientation and other factors, Dr. Uriarte and her team found.

ERIKA P. RODRIGUEZ FOR THE NEW YORK TIMES

Hurricane Maria's winds blew off much of the canopy cover, exposing the once-covered slopes of El Yunque.

They will eventually use the collected data, with the remote-sensing images and measurements, to come up with a detailed estimate of the loss from the storm.

The work is just getting started. The plan, Dr. Uriarte said, is to monitor the plots closely for several years and then less often, depending on funding.

While Dr. Uriarte doesn't know what her final conclusions will be, she has some ideas.

"One of the things that we are seeing in forests that get more severe hurricanes is that you end up with a shorter, smaller forest, which means less carbon overall," she said.

Whether that will happen here in Puerto Rico is one of the big questions.

"Are we going to lose some of the species? Are other species going to become more common?" she said. "We're trying to understand this variation, and part of that is recognizing how they respond to damage."

# Glossary

**agglomeration**  A large group of many different things collected or brought together.

**carbon emissions**  The carbon dioxide that planes, cars and factories produce, which is harmful to the environment.

**cistern**  A tank or underground reservoir that is used to store water.

**climate denialists**  People who deny the existence of climate change, or are skeptical about it.

**cognitive dissonance**  The mental discomfort or stress caused when a person holds two conflicting values, beliefs, or ideas.

**congruent**  The state of agreement, harmony, or compatibility.

**desertification**  The process when fertile, farmable land becomes desert, usually because of drought, deforestation or bad agricultural practices.

**ecosystem**  All the plants and animals that live in a particular area together, and the complex relationship that exists between them and their environment.

**encroachment**  The process of intruding into another person's territory or their rights.

**fissure**  A long narrow opening caused by cracking or splitting, especially in rock or earth.

**groundwater**  The water that is held underground in soil, or in the crevices or pores of rock.

**infrastructure**  The basic facilities and systems serving a country, city or area, such as transportation and communication systems, power plants and schools.

**jingoism**  Extreme patriotism, especially in the form of aggressive or warlike foreign policy.

**levee**  An embankment built to prevent river water from spilling out of its banks.

**lucrative**  Description of something that makes a great deal of money or profit.

**metropolis**  A very large, heavily populated, and busy city.

**precipitation**  The rain, snow, sleet or hail that falls to the ground.

**quixotic**  Description of something that is extremely foolish, unrealistic or idealistic.

**resilience**  Having or showing a sensible and practical idea of what can be achieved or expected.

**subsidy**  The money that is paid usually by a government to keep the price of a product or service low or to help a business or organization to continue to function.

**subsistence**  The minimal resources that are necessary for survival, without producing any surplus.

**xenophobia**  Showing dislike or prejudice towards people from other countries.

# Media Literacy Terms

"Media literacy" refers to the ability to access, understand, critically assess and create media. The following terms are important components of media literacy, and they will help you critically engage with the articles in this title.

**angle** The aspect of a news story that a journalist focuses on and develops.

**attribution** The method by which a source is identified or by which facts and information are assigned to the person who provided them.

**balance** Principle of journalism that both perspectives of an argument should be presented in a fair way.

**bias** A disposition of prejudice in favor of a certain idea, person, or perspective.

**byline** Name of the writer, usually placed between the headline and the story.

**commentary** Type of story that is an expression of opinion on recent events by a journalist generally known as a commentator.

**credibility** The quality of being trustworthy and believable, said of a journalistic source.

**editorial** Article of opinion or interpretation.

**feature story** Article designed to entertain as well as to inform.

**headline** Type, usually 18 point or larger, used to introduce a story.

**human interest story** Type of story that focuses on individuals and how events or issues affect their life, generally offering a sense of relatability to the reader.

**impartiality** Principle of journalism that a story should not reflect a journalist's bias and should contain balance.

**intention** The motive or reason behind something, such as the publication of a news story.

**motive** The reason behind something, such as the publication of a news story or a source's perspective on an issue.

**news story** An article or style of expository writing that reports news, generally in a straightforward fashion and without editorial comment.

**op-ed** An opinion piece that reflects a prominent individual's opinion on topic of interest.

**paraphrase** The summary of an individual's words, with attribution, rather than a direct quotation of their exact words.

**plagiarism** An attempt to pass another person's work as one's own without attribution.

**quotation** The use of an individual's exact words indicated by the use of quotation marks and proper attribution.

**reliability** The quality of being dependable and accurate, said of a journalistic source.

**rhetorical device** Technique in writing intending to persuade the reader or communicate a message from a certain perspective.

**source** The origin of the information reported in journalism.

**style** A distinctive use of language in writing or speech; also a news or publishing organization's rules for consistent use of language with regards to spelling, punctuation, typography, and capitalization, usually regimented by a house style guide.

**tone** A manner of expression in writing or speech.

# Media Literacy Questions

**1.** Identify the various sources cited in the article "Left to Louisiana's Tides, a Village Fights for Time" (on page 49). How does the journalist attribute information to each of these sources in their article? How effective are their attributions in helping the reader identify their sources?

**2.** In "Left to Louisiana's Tides, a Village Fights for Time" (on page 49), Tim Wallace and John Schwartz directly quote many residents of the town. What are the strengths of the use of a direct quote as opposed to a paraphrase? What are its weaknesses?

**3.** Compare the headlines of "Climate Change Is Driving People From Home. So Why Don't They Count as Refugees?" (on page 152) and "A Spy's Guide to Climate Change" (on page 159). Which is a more compelling headline, and why? How could the less compelling headline be changed to better draw the reader's interest?

**4.** What type of story is "Climate Change in My Backyard" (on page 91)? Can you identify another article in this collection that is the same type of story?

**5.** Does Nicholas Kristof demonstrate the journalistic principle of balance in his article "As Donald Trump Denies Climate Change, These Kids Die of It" (on page 143)? If so, how did he do this? If not, what could he have included to make his article more balanced?

**6.** The article "Running Dry in Cape Town" (on page 155) is an example of an op-ed. Identify how Dianna Kane's attitude, tone and perspective help convey her opinion on the topic.

**7.** Does "Mexico City, Parched and Sinking, Faces a Water Crisis" (on page 20) use multiple sources? What are the strengths of using multiple sources in a journalistic piece? What are the weaknesses of relying heavily on only one source?

**8.** "Left to Louisiana's Tides, a Village Fights for Time" (on page 49) features many photographs of life in this town. What do these photographs add to the article?

**9.** What is the intention of the article "What Land Will Be Underwater in 20 Years? Figuring It Out Could Be Lucrative" (on page 197)? How effectively does it achieve its intended purpose?

**10.** Analyze the reporting in "As Climate Changes, Southern States Will Suffer More Than Others" (on page 87) and "Climate Change Is Driving People From Home. So Why Don't They Count as Refugees?" (on page 152). Do you think one article is more balanced and thorough than the other? If so, why do you think so?

**11.** Identify each of the sources in "Drought and War Heighten Threat of Not Just 1 Famine, But 4" (on page 95) as a primary source or a secondary source. Evaluate the reliability and credibility of each source. How does your evaluation of each source change your perspective on this article?

# Citations

All citations in this list are formatted according to the Modern Language Association's (MLA) style guide.

## BOOK CITATION

NEW YORK TIMES EDITORIAL STAFF, THE. *Climate Refugees: How Climate Change Is Displacing Millions*. New York: New York Times Educational Publishing, 2019.

## ARTICLE CITATIONS

AHMED, K. ANIS. "In Bangladesh, a Flood and an Efficient Response." *The New York Times*, 1 Sept. 2017, https://www.nytimes.com/2017/09/01/opinion/bangladesh-floods.html.

ASTOR, MAGGIE. "No Children Because of Climate Change? Some People Are Considering It." *The New York Times*, 05 Feb. 2018, https://www.nytimes.com/2018/02/05/climate/climate-change-children.html.

BENKO, JESSICA. "How a Warming Planet Drives Human Migration." *The New York Times*, 19 Apr. 2017, https://www.nytimes.com/2017/04/19/magazine/how-a-warming-planet-drives-human-migration.html.

BROMWICH, JONAH ENGEL. "Where Can You Escape the Harshest Effects of Climate Change?" *The New York Times*, 20 Oct. 2016, https://www.nytimes.com/2016/10/20/science/9-cities-to-live-in-if-youre-worried-about-climate-change.html.

CASEY, NICHOLAS. "A Lifetime in Peru's Glaciers, Slowly Melting Away." *The New York Times*, 26 Jan. 2018, https://www.nytimes.com/2018/01/26/world/americas/peru-glaciers-andes-melting.html.

CASEY, NICHOLAS. "Climate Change Claims a Lake, and an Identity." *The New York Times*, 7 July 2016, https://www.nytimes.com/interactive/2016/07/07/world/americas/bolivia-climate-change-lake-poopo.html.

DAVENPORT, CORAL, AND CAMPBELL ROBERTSON. "Resettling the First American 'Climate Refugees'." *The New York Times*, 3 May 2016, https://www.nytimes.com/2016/05/03/us/resettling-the-first-american-climate-refugees.html.

FOUNTAIN, HENRY. "Forests Protect the Climate. A Future With More Storms Would Mean Trouble." *The New York Times*, 7 Mar. 2018, https://www.nytimes.com/2018/03/07/climate/forests-storms-climate-change.html.

GETTLEMAN, JEFFREY. "Drought and War Heighten Threat of Not Just 1 Famine, but 4." *The New York Times*, 27 Mar. 2017, https://www.nytimes.com/2017/03/27/world/africa/famine-somalia-nigeria-south-sudan-yemen-water.html.

GILLIS, JUSTIN. "The Real Unknown of Climate Changes: Our Behavior." *The New York Times*, 18 Sept. 2017, https://www.nytimes.com/2017/09/18/climate/climate-change-denial.html.

GILLIS, JUSTIN. "A Spy's Guide to Climate Change." *The New York Times*, 15 Feb. 2018, https://www.nytimes.com/2018/02/15/opinion/guide-climate-change.html.

GOODE, ERICA. "Polar Bears' Path to Decline Runs Through Alaskan Village." *The New York Times*, 18 Dec. 2016, https://www.nytimes.com/2016/12/18/science/polar-bears-global-warming.html.

GOODE, ERICA. "A Wrenching Choice for Alaska Towns in the Path of Climate Change." *The New York Times*, 29 Nov. 2016, https://www.nytimes.com/interactive/2016/11/29/science/alaska-global-warming.html.

HANER, JOSH, ET AL. "Living in China's Expanding Deserts." *The New York Times*, 24 Oct. 2016, https://www.nytimes.com/interactive/2016/10/24/world/asia/living-in-chinas-expanding-deserts.html.

IVES, MIKE. "A Remote Pacific Nation, Threatened by Rising Seas." *The New York Times*, 2 July 2016, https://www.nytimes.com/2016/07/03/world/asia/climate-change-kiribati.html.

KANE, DIANNA. "Running Dry in Cape Town." *The New York Times*, 1 Feb. 2017, https://www.nytimes.com/2018/02/01/opinion/cape-town-drought-day-zero.html.

KIMMELMAN, MICHAEL. "Mexico City, Parched and Sinking, Faces a Water Crisis." *The New York Times*, 17 Feb. 2017, https://www.nytimes.com/interactive/2017/02/17/world/americas/mexico-city-sinking.html.

KRISTOF, NICHOLAS. "As Donald Trump Denies Climate Change, These Kids Die of It." *The New York Times*, 6 Jan. 2017, https://www.nytimes.com/2017/

01/06/opinion/sunday/as-donald-trump-denies-climate-change-these-kids
-die-of-it.html.

KRISTOF, NICHOLAS. "Swallowed by the Sea." *The New York Times*, 19 Jan. 2018,
https://www.nytimes.com/2018/01/19/opinion/sunday/climate-change
-bangladesh.html.

PELTIER, ELIAN, AND ELOISE STARK. "Floods Leave Paris Contemplating a
Wetter Future." *The New York Times*, 26 Jan. 2018, https://www.nytimes
.com/2018/01/26/world/europe/france-paris-floods.html.

PIERRE-LOUIS, KENDRA, AND NADJA POPOVICH. "Of 21 Winter Olympic Cities,
Many May Soon Be Too Warm to Host the Games." *The New York Times*, 11
Jan. 2018, https://www.nytimes.com/interactive/2018/01/11/climate/winter
-olympics-global-warming.html.

PLUMER, BRAD. "What Land Will Be Underwater in 20 Years? Figuring It Out
Could Be Lucrative." *The New York Times*, 23 Feb. 2018, https://www
.nytimes.com/2018/02/23/climate/mapping-future-climate-risk.html.

PLUMER, BRAD, AND NADJA POPOVICH. "As Climate Changes, Southern States
Will Suffer More Than Others." *The New York Times*, 29 June 2017, https://
www.nytimes.com/interactive/2017/06/29/climate/southern-states-worse
-climate-effects.html.

RYTZ, MATTHIEU. "Sinking Islands, Floating Nation." *The New York Times*, 24
Jan. 2018, https://www.nytimes.com/2018/01/24/opinion/kiribati-climate
-change.html.

SCHWARTZ, JOHN. "Providing for 7 Billion. Or Not." *The New York Times*, 14
Feb. 2018, https://www.nytimes.com/2018/02/14/climate/sustainable
-good-life.html.

SCHWARTZ, JOHN, AND MARK SCHLEIFSTEIN. "Fortified But Still In Peril, New
Orleans Braces For Its Future." *The New York Times*, 24 Feb. 2018, https://
www.nytimes.com/interactive/2018/02/24/us/new-orleans-flood-walls
-hurricanes.html.

SENGUPTA, SOMINI. "Climate Change Is Driving People From Home. So Why
Don't They Count as Refugees?" *The New York Times*, 21 Dec. 2017, https://
www.nytimes.com/2017/12/21/climate/climate-refugees.html.

SENGUPTA, SOMINI. "Heat, Hunger and War Force Africans Onto a 'Road on
Fire'." *The New York Times*, 15 Dec. 2016, https://www.nytimes.com/
interactive/2016/12/15/world/africa/agadez-climate-change.html.

SENGUPTA, SOMINI. "Warming, Water Crisis, Then Unrest: How Iran Fits an
Alarming Pattern." *The New York Times*, 18 Jan. 2018, https://www.nytimes

.com/2018/01/18/climate/water-iran.html.

STOKES, LEAH C. "Climate Change in My Backyard." *The New York Times*, 11 Jan. 2018, https://www.nytimes.com/2018/01/11/opinion/california-floods -mudslides-climate.html.

WALLACE, TIM, AND JOHN SCHWARTZ. "Left to Louisiana's Tides, a Village Fights for Time." *The New York Times*, 24 Feb, 2018, https://www.nytimes .com/interactive/2018/02/24/us/jean-lafitte-floodwaters.html.

WONG, EDWARD. "Resettling China's 'Ecological Migrants'." *The New York Times*, 25 Oct. 2016, https://www.nytimes.com/interactive/2016/10/25/ world/asia/china-climate-change-resettlement.html.

# Index